The Inheritance

The Inheritance

J B Dunlop

THE INHERATANCE

Editor: Kimberly Mathews
Cover Design: B A Trimmer
ISBN-13: 978-1099257933
Dunlop Productions, Manchester, United Kingdom
060119

E-mail the author at jbdunlop22@hotmail.com

To Steve Mckeown who died on 3rd of January 2019.
Half of the proceeds from this book will be donated to the Heart
Foundation in his memory.
My very dear friend who will forever be remembered.

Thanks to Steve and Ang McKeown for the use of their home for most of this book, and for their constant support.
Thanks to Tracey Purdham for being my sounding board.
Thanks to B. A. Trimmer (Author) for his guidance.
Thanks to our Joanne (Ward) and Lorraine Newton (BF) for their never-ending love and friendship.

The
Inheritance

ONE

"Well, that's it," I said, turning to my best friend and her husband.

"Are you sure this is what you really want to do?" Alice asked.

"Yes, I really need to do this."

Zuess, my blue staff, whimpered from the passenger side of my blue soft-top Beetle, in which all my worldly possessions were packed.

"But you don't even know where you're going," Alice said. "Why would someone you've never even met leave you a cottage, in the middle of nowhere, at the other end of the country? I've never even heard of Glenwillow. It's so far away from everyone you care about."

"Look, what do I have to lose? My boss sold the company, then retired. I practically ran the business for the last three years, then he took it all away. I'm not comfortable working for a large international company again. I don't want to go back to being someone's lackey. I've moved on since those days. Besides, you, Adam, and little Matt here are my family and you're only a phone call away. You're coming to visit soon, yes? You did promise."

"I know, but I worry about you. You know what you're like for getting yourself into trouble," Alice said.

"You mean like the time I pressed the emergency button in the plane toilets and started a panic?" I asked with a grin. "Or the time I locked myself in the pub toilet and you didn't even know I was missing until an hour after last orders? As for the someone I never met, she was my grandmother. Granted my mother did forget to mention her, but I still need to do this."

Zuess started whining again with impatience and I turned to Alice. "Look, I must get going. I don't want to get caught in the works traffic. My mobile is on and I'll ring you when I get there safely."

Alice grabbed me in a bear hug.

"I love you, Molly. Ring me each stop so I know you're safe."

I hugged Adam, then lifted my godson Matt off his feet and hugged him hard. I gave him a big wet kiss on the cheek, the kind all children hate. He giggled and wiped his cheek as I set him down.

"Right," I said. "Here goes." I turned and jumped in my car before the tears that threatened started to fall.

"Off we go, Zuess. Our new life begins today."

As we headed down the road, I watched in the rear-view mirror as my best friend and her family became dots on the horizon.

TWO

Six hours later, sun shining, top down, and Ed Sheeran singing to us through the radio, we pulled in to a little village called Glenwillow. My sat-nav, Tim, said I was very near my destination, so me and Zuess decided we needed to scope out the little shop in town and pick up some necessaries – red wine, doggy chews, bread and cheese. I'd brought my store cupboard with me, but not any fresh stuff. I thought I'd familiarize myself with the local shop on the way in.

Now, how to do this, I thought, as there didn't seem to be anyone about. Should I leave Zeuss in the car to dart into the shop? If he saw another dog, he'd be off who knows where. Or, should I put the top up just to make sure he stays put. Decisions. Decisions.

"Right, Zeussy, let's put your lead on. I need to go in the shop and they don't allow dogs, so I'm going to tie you to that pole over there." I always talk to my dog because there's just me and him and he's the only one that thinks I make sense most of the time.

"Stay, Zuess and be good." I turned and entered the quaint little shop that appeared to stock just about everything.

"Hello. Can I help you?" a friendly fifty-something-year-old gentleman beamed at me from over the counter.

"Yes, please. I'd like a nice bottle of red wine, fresh bread, doggy treats, some butter, and cheese. Oh, and you better add milk to that list."

"I think we can just about manage that young lady. Are you staying local?"

"Molly," I said as I leaned over the counter and shook the gentleman's hand.

"Albert," he said as he smiled back at me.

"Nice to meet you, Albert. I'm moving into the area. My grandmother passed away and left me her house, not far from here, so I decided to leave the humdrum life of the north and start a whole new chapter here in your lovely countryside."

"Ah, you must be Francesca's granddaughter then?"

"Yes, that's right. She talked about me? I never met her. To be honest I was a bit shocked not only to find out that I had a grandmother, but that she had left everything to me when she passed over."

"She talked about you all the time. She was proud of you. Is that your dog outside?"

"Yes." I dashed to the door to make sure Zuessy was where I left him.

"Nice dog. Blue staff if I'm not mistaken." Albert shouted from the back of the shop. He was obviously gathering my order together.

Turning, I made my way back to the counter just as Albert returned, his arms full, and started packing a carrier bag.

"Do you want me to start a tab?" he asked. "Or do you want to pay as you go along?"

"Oh, people still have tabs?" I laughed.

Albert laughed too. "They do around here; it's very rural. We all know one another, so there is a lot of trust."

"I think I'm going to love living here, Albert." I paid, collected my shopping, and moved towards the door.

"See you soon, Albert. Come along, Zuess. Time to find home."

THREE

"You have now reached your destination," Tim said in his sexy American accent. I pulled to the side of the road, beside the most beautiful cottage, complete with a white picket fence.

"Oh my God, Zeuss, look at that. This must be a mistake."

The roof was thatched and was sculptured at the top, with two bedroom windows inset. The front had some kind of climber with beautiful pink flowers that were in full bloom. The garden was immaculate – someone had obviously been looking after it since grandma had died. You couldn't see the soil for flowers of every color combination. The door was bright red with a shiny brass knocker.

"Oh! My giddy aunt, this is absolutely fab!" I whispered to myself.

Something white caught my eye, about the same time it also caught Zuess's eye.

"NO! NO! NO!" I shouted.

But it was too late. Zuess jumped from the front seat to the back, and then over the top, going sixty miles an hour. He slammed through the gate, which was off the latch, with me in hot pursuit. As I pushed the gate and ran through, my foot caught on something and I face planted into the nearest rose bush. I heard a lot of snapping noises before my nose hit the soil. I lowered my head, closed my eyes, and then waited for the sounds of murder, as my dog ate the unsuspecting animal. Nothing, not a sound, until I heard a door slam.

A horrible thought suddenly struck me. Oh my God! I do hope this is the right house.

The gate squeaked. "Miss? Miss are you alright?" a young voice asked.

Oh my God, so embarrassing. I looked up to find a little boy standing in front of me.

"Hello!" I said.

"Hello! I'm James," the boy said.

"I'm Molly," I answered.

"Are you Francesca's granddaughter?" He asked me as he lowered to his knees, peering into my face.

At that moment, a deep male voice called out from behind me. "James, what are you doing?"

I turned my head to the side noticing a very large pair of shoes, which were obviously very, very, expensive. My head tilted upwards to a never-ending pair of legs covered in very well-cut suit trousers.

His hair was as black as coal and he had rugged good looks, sporting designer stubble. My neck was aching, so I thought it was best to stand to get a better look at this Adonis, if the bottom half was anything to go by. I put my hands in front of me and gradually brought my knees up, so that I could make a more lady like stand.

"Alexander, this is Molly," James said. He turned to me saying, "Molly, this is my uncle, Alexander."

After gracefully getting to my feet, I turned towards Alexander only to find that my eyes were on a level with his chest. I took a step back and tilted my head backwards once again. At this point I think I swallowed the wrong way because I erupted into a fit of coughing.

"Oh dear," I said, apologizing. I held my hand out to introduce myself properly. If nothing else, I've manners, and it gave me a chance to hold the hand of this god-like creature.

"You're very tall." Oh my God, did I just say that out loud?

"Six foot one," he said, smirking.

"Oh!" I answered, shaking my head to wake my brain up so that my mouth would work. "Am I at the right house?"

"Yes, Molly, you are," he laughed.

Just as I was about to respond, we both heard the distant rumble of a very powerful motor bike. Alex mumbled something under his breath that sounded Italian to my untrained ear.

Interesting that English wasn't his native tongue. Although he looked English to me, but what did I know?

The noisy machine stopped in front of us. The passenger sleekly dismounted, pulling his helmet off as he came to a stop next to Alexander.

"Alexander," the stranger nodded at him as he said his name.

He was as tall as Alexander and muscle-bound, however he was blond. They both looked as though they worked out in a gym. Where there would be a gym in this neck of the woods was a mystery, because it looked like all cows and fields to me.

"I'm Kade. Hello, you must be Molly." As he introduced himself, he shook my hand.

"Kade," Alexander nodded to the stranger then went off at a tangent speaking in that Italian lingo again.

"Excuse me, gentlemen, I don't want to interrupt, but can you just look to see if you can find my dog? And has he got something dead in his mouth?" Their conversation abruptly stopped as they looked behind me, then back at me.

"Your dog is fine, and he seems to have found a new friend, well two actually." Kade laughed. I turned to see what had him amused. To my utter amazement, Zeuss was lying on his back having his tummy rubbed by James, whilst sniffing the face of the most beautiful long-haired white cat I've ever seen.

"Unreal!" I muttered and stumbled over to the front step, dropping to my knees to stroke this new addition to our growing numbers. At this rate we could have a party.

"Hello there, my lovely, what is your name?"

James spoke up, "This is Missy, Francesca's, I mean your grandmother's cat."

"Oh." I seemed to be saying that a lot since I arrived. "It's a good job Zuess likes Missy then, because it could have gotten a bit messy," I laughed. Funny, grandma's solicitor never mentioned Missy. Anyway, I didn't have time for all the fraternizing; I had things to do. I turned and looked over my shoulder to see what was happening. The men were deep in conversation, having lost interest in the menagerie on the door step. There didn't seem to be any love lost between them I noticed.

"Right, James," I said. "I think I need to unpack the car and have a look around. How old are you?"

"I'm eight," James said with pride.

"Wow, you're nearly a man. How would you like to help me unpack and have a look around my new home, seeing as you already seem to know so much about it? Where do you live by the way?"

"Next door, behind that big wall." He turned and pointed.

"My, that's quite a wall, how come you have to have a wall that tall?" I asked.

"My grandfather is an important man in Italy, so he has a lot of security," James answered.

"You don't sound Italian to me," I said.

"No, I go to boarding school here in England. I come and stay with Grandfather in the summer holidays."

"You seem very grown up for eight," I said.

James laughed. "I like you, Molly. Will you be my friend?"

"I'd love to," I answered.

We left Zuess and Missy as they got better acquainted, which spooked me out because Zuess was definitely not an animal-friendly kind of guy. Something to ponder on later.

The two hunks had moved near to Alexander's car, which, by the way, was very sporty, very black, and very sexy.

"What's the history with the two of them, James?" I asked.

"Not sure. I think it's got something to do with Grandfather's business. I try to listen, but they always shoo me away."

"Okay then. Should I open the door and have a look at my new home? Come on, Zuess, Missy."

In we trooped.

"Oh my God, I'm stunned, it's absolutely beautiful. So oldy-worldly and quaint. Oh, James, I'm going to love it here," I said with a big grin on my face.

The front door led into a very spacious living room with a soft cushion settee in egg-shell blue, with loads of scatter cushions. The fireplace was original with wood beams that surrounded a log burner. There was a dresser in the corner with old china plates and tea sets, and in the opposite corner, was a flat screen TV with a sound system. The floor was wooden with rugs that matched the settee and scatter cushions. Wooden beams ran along the ceiling and beautiful paintings hung on the walls.

I walked through a door that led into a kitchen to die for. It was massive with an electric range set in an island in the center, fully fitted cupboards in white, with lemon walls, a double fridge/freezer American-style, and a breakfast bar. Over in the corner was a dining table that sat six, made with oak. There were two doors leading off the room. I opened one that led to a laundry room, then opened the other to find a fully stocked pantry.

"James, I'm in love," I whispered. He giggled but remained silent.

I heard voices in the other room. I ruffled James's head and returned to the living room to find Alexander and Kade trooping in with boxes out of the car.

"Oh, thank you, you didn't have to do that. I'm sure you both have somewhere to be," I said with a smile.

"No," they both said looking at each other, then at me.

"Well I haven't brought much, so I can take it from here. But thank you both once again."

"You don't seem to have a lot with you, considering you're moving in," Alexander said with raised eyebrows.

"No. New start, so I only brought my art and my clothes. Mr. Ellis said I wouldn't need anything because my grandmother had everything I'd need," I replied.

"Mr. Ellis?" Kade asked.

"Mr. Ellis is, was, my grandmother's adviser."

"You paint?" Kade enquired.

"No, not really. I'm learning. I'm mainly a sketcher. I cook and bake, and I write a little. However, I'm an accountant by trade. Oh, and I like gardening and listening to music. I feel like I'm auditioning for a chat show," I laughed. "What do you do for a living?" I asked.

"I could tell you, but I'd have to kill you," Kade said.

I swear Alexander growled at his reply.

"Oh," I said, frowning. There was that word again, I seemed to be saying it a lot. Turning to Alexander, I asked, "And what do you do for a living?"

"I work with my father."

Well, two very interesting professions (not). I was no further along in knowing what either of them did for a living.

"Well, like I said, thank you, but I do need to start unpacking and finding my way around." I looked around but couldn't find either Zuess or Missy. Muttering to myself, I opened the back door to locate my dog and his new friend.

"Zuess! Missy! Come on in, dinner time," I shouted.

That's if I could locate some, I thought.

When I turned around, Kade had disappeared and Alexander was persuading James to return to the car.

"Molly, can I come around to help you? You know, do the garden and stuff. I get lonely in the summer holidays," James said.

"Of course, James. Any time you want to, however, you must always tell someone where you are, so they don't worry."

"I know. Grandfather's rules are very strict."

"Then we have a deal," I said.

Alexander gently pushed James through the front door. Turning to me he said, "Nice to finally meet you, Molly. I hope to see a lot of you."

With that he kissed both my cheeks and left.

I watched as they pulled away, made sure my car was locked and the soft top was up before returning to the cottage, locking the door behind me.

FOUR

I woke to the morning chorus of birds, having decided last night to leave the unpacking, which wasn't much. It had been a long day, I'm not a confident driver, so I was beat from the six-hour drive, and a bit overwhelmed by my house and guests.

I'd found the bathroom the night before, spacious and modern, with a double walk in shower, a bath tub on legs, and there were even fluffy matching towels on the radiator. It felt as though my grandmother had just stepped out to the shops – the house felt lived in, cozy and warm.

I quickly had a shower and dressed in jeans and a t-shirt, making my way downstairs to feed Zuess and my new cat Missy. It was a beautiful sunny day. I opened the windows in the living room and kitchen, leaving the back door open to let in the cool breeze. I then let my pets out for their morning rituals. I rooted in the boxes I'd brought looking for the base station for my phone, plugging it in to play some music.

Taking my freshly made cup of tea, I wandered outside, finding a little iron patio set for two. Sitting down, I watched the animals sniff around the garden for hidden treasures. The garden was as beautiful as the cottage, well thought out, green and colorful, with the flower beds in full bloom. At the bottom was a greenhouse with what looked like tomatoes, lettuce, and onions growing. It also had a little shed off to the side, which I assumed housed the lawn equipment. To be so lucky, I thought, to be gifted this from a grandmother I didn't know existed, was just unbelievable. I closed my eyes and listened to Rag'n'Bone Man singing from the kitchen, lost in thought.

My thoughts drifted back to my dream from the night before, the dream that included two totally naked six-foot odd Italian stallions, full of muscle and tattoos. Where the tattoos came from I'd no idea, I don't even like them. I definitely had no idea whether Kade or Alexander had any, but it would be fun to find out. Even though I was alone, I could feel myself blushing. I should really get my thoughts out of the gutter. Never in my life have I had sexy dreams about one man before, never mind two.

I jumped when I heard a noise, opening my eyes. "Hey, guys, did you hear that humming?" Both animals sat on the grass, looking at me with innocent eyes. "You heard it, didn't you?" I frowned at them but got no answer and the humming had stopped.

"Molly! Molly! Can I come in?" a little voice shouted from the side gate.

"James! Is that you?" I shouted back.

"Yes, Molly, can I come in?"

"Yes, of course." I jumped up and made my way to the gate where James was wrestling with the catch. "Gosh, you're up and about early. Are you on your own?"

"Yes. Alexander is busy today with business, so I thought I could help you unpack, and watch you draw and paint. Will you teach me?"

I laughed, giving his hair a ruffle. "I'm sure you're better than me. Have you had breakfast yet?"

"No, I was so excited to see you again and Zuess and Missy, I forgot," he said.

"Well we should start by cooking breakfast together, then we'll see where the day takes us."

14

Zuess zealously welcomed our new guest then wondered off, so James and I both went to investigate the pantry.

"Well, James, it's definitely well stocked. I wonder who did this for me?" I pondered out loud.

"Probably Kade," James said coming up behind me.

"Why would he do that?" I asked.

"Well, when your grandmother became ill, he looked after her, you know, like cutting the garden and doing her shopping."

"Oh, okay. I'll have to ask him how much I owe him for getting my groceries. Now, how do you fancy a boiled egg and soldiers?" I asked.

"What's soldiers, Molly?"

I laughed and teased him. "Soldiers. You don't know what soldiers are?" I ruffled his hair. "Soldiers are a slice of toast cut into strips, then dunked into your egg. I think we're going to have to broaden your education. Don't you have breakfast at this fancy school of yours?"

"Yes, Molly, but we have cereal or bacon and eggs."

"Very nice, you're spoiled," I laughed.

After breakfast and a clean-up, we found the keys to the shed and went to investigate. As I opened the door, both animals dived in like scouts on a mission. "Ok, guys! Out now, let us in." Zuess grumbled and Missy sauntered out, leaving James and me to wander and investigate the contents.

"Hey, James, there's a bike here. How about you teach me to ride?"

"Wow, Molly. You've never ridden a bike?" he asked in wonder.

Laughing, I answered. "Well yes, but it was a very long time ago, when I was a little girl."

"Okay, Molly, I'll bring my bike over tomorrow and we'll go for a ride."

"Cool," I answered.

Just then there was a lot of commotion outside, and the side gate rattled as it was opened.

"James! James! Are you here?" A deep voice shouted angrily. I jumped a mile, dropped what I was holding, and fell outside the shed door.

"Who are you?" I said, shielding James with my slight frame, all five foot four, or two, of it. Ignoring me, he shouted again with authority making even me cower.

"Who are you and why are you shouting?" I asked, raising my voice to be heard.

"I'm looking for my grandson."

"Oh!" I turned, grabbing James' hand in mine. "Well, he's here." I turned to the boy. "James! Did you not tell anyone were you were going? I thought we agreed on this."

"Sorry. Alexander was on a business call and I couldn't find Jacob," he answered timidly.

"Who's Jacob?" I whispered. James pointed to the giant of a man dressed in a black suit and black tie standing next to his grandfather.

"He is."

"Oh. They make the men big around here don't they?" I observed. Jacob turned his head away with a smirk on his face, which he was obviously trying to hide. James' grandfather stepped forward with his hand out.

"Molly, I presume? Nice to meet you. I'm very sorry for scaring you and shouting. James has been told on numerous occasions not to leave the grounds alone. I thought something had happened to him." His tone had turned friendly and sincere. Even though the older man

16

was in his late sixties, he was still tall and attractive. He had an air of authority about him, a man not to be crossed.

"I understand. We discussed this last night with your son Alexander. James assured me he'd tell someone when he came over. I'm so sorry."

"That's okay, Molly. No harm done this time. James, come along. We need to have a man-to-man chat." Turning to me, James' grandfather took my shoulders, placing a kiss on each cheek. "Molly, nice to finally meet you. I'm sure we'll be seeing a lot of each other." Turning he said, "James, come." Jacob nodded to me as he turned to follow them out the side gate.

Well that was interesting, I thought. However, I didn't have time to ponder as my mobile started singing Michael Bublé at me. "Oh shit! Shit! Shit!" I totally forgot to check in with Alice last night, and this morning. I hadn't even checked if I'd had any missed calls; she's not going to be pleased.

I snatched up my mobile before it went to voicemail. "Molly! Molly! is that you? Thank God. I was so worried. I was about to report you missing," my best friend said.

"Oh my God, Alice. I've so much to tell you. I'm so, so, sorry for not checking in, but, oh God, I met two hotties last night, and this adorable little boy called James, who asked me to be his friend and I just couldn't refuse, and the house, oh my God, it's incredible, and James came around this morning, we found a bike in the shed, James is going to teach me to ride, so we can go on bike rides together, did I mention the cat, God she's so adorable, she's white and long-haired and Zuess just loves her, they're inseparable." I finally stopped to catch my breath.

"Slow down, Molly. I can't take it all in. Start at the two hotties," she laughed.

"Well, Alexander, is so tall and muscly, dark and handsome. He's James' uncle from the house next door that's surrounded by a huge wall. I think they're Italian because I heard him speak to Kade in Italian. Don't know where he lives, but he arrived on the biggest bike you ever did see. He's as tall as Alexander, just as muscly but blond, looks like he could be special forces. Apparently, he helped Grandma when she was ill, stocked the fridge and larder. God I must talk to him about that; I'll need to reimburse him. Oh God! And there's James' grandfather, looks a bit like a mafia boss and his minder Jacob. He's a bit of a hottie, too."

"Well! you're okay then?" she laughed and continued. "Molly, I've got to go, I've an appointment. I'm just so glad you answered the phone. Adam and I were getting so worried. Please stay in touch and ring me with the gossip. Please stay safe and we'll speak soon."

"Okay," I answered. "Love you. Take good care of that godson of mine," I said as the phone clicked off.

I docked my phone to recharge and listen to some music, looking around for my pets, and finding them sound asleep in a huddle. I then went to investigate the freezer, which again was fully stocked. Thrilled with the chance to cook, I pulled out some very healthy-looking mince for a bolognaise and some frozen pastry to make a quiche. I grabbed my sketch pad, pencils and rubber, and set up on the table outside. I looked at the clock. Three o'clock. Good time for a wine and some down time.

FIVE

I lose track of time when I'm drawing, and by the time I looked up, the sun had gone down, and the light was fading fast. Time to move inside. Zuess and Missy were whining. "Okay guys, tea time." After feeding the animals, I popped the surround sound system to play, poured a glass of red, and started preparing my spaghetti bolognaise and quiche for tomorrow. That's when I noticed the humming sound again. I stopped what I was doing, found the remote and turned the sound really low, but the humming had disappeared again. "Odd, really odd," I whispered.

The next thing, Zuess jumped up and ran to the back door with his tail wagging, Missy ran after him meowing. There was a double rap on the door. Leaving the music turned low, I followed the animals, opening the door before my visitor could knock again.

"Molly." Kade stood on the door step holding a bottle of red wine and a frown. "Do you normally answer the door without checking who it is first? I could have been anyone. What if you were attacked or robbed? You could have been here days before some-one found you."

Raising my eyebrows, I said, "Gosh, that's a bit over-dramatic, Kade. Is this a bad area? Mr. Ellis never mentioned it was rough. Besides that, either you or Alexander are always around. It's as though you have some kind of homing device on me."

"No, Molly, it's not, but you need to be a bit more careful living in the country. It's a lot different than living in a town or city."

I smiled. "Well are you coming in, or just going to stand there. I'm cooking and I need to check things before they burn." Turning, I headed back to the stove, grabbing my wine on the way.

"Something smells good," he said moving behind me and leaning over my shoulder. I felt myself getting all hot and bothered.

"Errr… spaghetti bolognaise. Would you like to share some? Or there's homemade quiche." He was so close, I could feel his breath on my neck and I was beetroot red.

"Would you mind? I'm starving, and it smells really good. Here, a house warming present." He handed me a bottle of red.

"Take a seat. It will take another hour. I took the meat out quite late in the day, and it's only just defrosted," I mumbled. God, this guy was so hot, I could feel butterflies in my stomach. He stepped away, moving to the table where I'd left my sketchbook.

"God, Molly, this is really good. How long have you been drawing?" He started flicking through the pages.

I popped the lid on the pan on a low flame and checked the pie in the oven before I answered.

"Around six months," I said.

"I thought you were going to say, since you were a child."

"No, I'm fairly new at it. Didn't know I could draw until a close friend who happens to be an artist encouraged me. I've done one term at night school, and then this happened. I mean a grandmother I didn't know existed left me this beautiful house, and now here I am."

"So, what have you got planned for the future?" he asked.

"Where's your helmet?"

"I walked. I only live around the corner; the house set back from the road."

"Oh! I didn't notice. I was so focused on Tim," I said.

"Tim?"

"My sat-nav."

With that, he laughed out loud.

"You didn't answer my question. What do you have planned?"

"Well, I haven't really planned that far. I've some money saved and Grandmother left me enough to live off for quite some time. However, I thought I'd set a stall up out front to sell some fruit and veg, maybe some of my drawings. I've some clients who I still bookkeep for. Instead of doing them for free, I thought I could charge a small fee, something they can afford."

"You're staying then? Not going to sell up and move on?"

"Wasn't planning on doing, selling, that is. Why should I be?" I said frowning.

"No. I'd like to get to know you better. Have you another glass? I think I'll try some of that wine."

"Oh my. I'm so sorry. I never offered. That's so rude of me." I stood up to retrieve a glass from the cupboard. Another knock sounded at the door. Before Kade could move. I rushed to open it.

"Alexander, come in. What can I do for you?" I stepped back to let him in.

"Molly, you should get a chain fitted on this bloody door. It's not safe to just open it to anyone," he said frowning. He stepped in, unaware of Kade sitting at the table.

"That's what I said," Kade spoke up.

"Kade? What are you doing here?"

"Presumably, the same as you." They both glared at each other.

"Well, this is cozy," I said raising my eyebrows. "I've just made supper Alexander, would you like some spaghetti bolognaise? Obviously not how your mother used to make, more a Molly special."

"Why not?" He smiled at Kade. Kade just raised his eyebrows and frowned.

"I'll get another glass then, or are you driving?"

"Oh, that reminds me, Molly, I've something for you." He delved into his pocket and brought out a bottle of red wine. "A welcome present, and no I'm not driving, I walked."

"Interesting." I looked at both and smiled. Turning, I reached into the cupboard and retrieved another glass, filling it with wine, and handing it to Alexander.

"Excuse me gentlemen, I need to sort the rest of supper." I reached for the remote, turned the music up, and left them talking. I guessed they didn't want me to know what it was about because they reverted to Italian again. I became so engrossed cooking, I forgot they were even in the room. I sang along with the music while I busied myself making salad, garlic bread, and boiled the water for the spaghetti. Every now and again, I noticed my wine glass refilled itself.

Thirty minutes later, everything was ready for serving. As I placed the dishes on the table for them to help themselves, I noticed the table had now been set. Just then my mobile rang.

"Hi!" I answered.

"Molly, how are you? What are you up to?" asked Alice.

"Cooking!"

"Cooking?" she said. "Have you got company?"

"Might have."

"Which one?"

"How do you even know that?"

"I just know. I've known you like forever. I can tell when you're out of your comfort zone."

"Both," I chuckled.

"Oh my God, do you want me to go?"

"Yes. Can I call you tomorrow? We're just about to eat," I stuttered.

"You can bet on it," she laughed out loud. "I love you, speak soon."

"I love you, too," but the phone had already gone dead.

I put the phone down, to find both men looking at me expectantly.

"A friend. You're hungry. Supper's ready," I said sitting down.

We ate in silence, not sure whether it was just manners, or whether my two guests were waiting for the other to start a conversation.

"That was delicious. Can I've some more?"

I laughed. "Sure, fill your boots." I leaned back in my chair and watched both Alexander and Kade spoon more food onto their plates.

"I met your father today," I said looking at Alexander.

"I believe so. He was angry with James because he ran off without telling anyone."

"So I heard and I scolded him about that. We found a bike in the garden shed. He said he'd teach me to ride it tomorrow. Will he be allowed to come here again?"

"I don't see why not. If Jacob watches over him," he said between bites as he dug into his second, or was it third, helping.

"Are you enjoying that?" I smirked.

"God, yes! It's the best thing I've ever tasted."

"I doubt that," I giggled. "But thank you. Why?"

"Why what?" He stopped eating and frowned at me.

"Why does James have to have a bodyguard, aka, Jacob?" I asked.

Before he could answer, Kade stepped in." Because Alexander and his father keep bad company, and James could become a target, and by association so could you." Alexander just glared at Kade and continued to eat. "Hence the need to put a secure lock and chain on your door."

"So, that explains both your visits this evening?"

"No, I like you and want to get to know you better," Kade answered.

"I came to explain about James, but now that I've discovered that you're an excellent cook, I'd also like to get to know you better." Alexander smiled, as he grabbed my hand and kissed it.

Kade grunted, putting his knife and fork down, obviously having had his fill of food.

I stood, collecting the now spotless plates and carried them to the sink. Kade followed with the empty dishes.

"More wine anyone?" I asked.

Just then Alexander's mobile rang. He answered abruptly, "Yes?" Followed by silence, as he listened. "Contain the problem. I'll be there in thirty minutes." He disconnected. "Sorry, Molly, I've to go."

"No problem. I hope everything's okay?"

"I'm sure Kade will help with the cleaning up. He then grabbed me by the shoulders planting a kiss on both cheeks, nodded at Kade and left, closing the door softly behind him. I just stood there flabbergasted.

"Well," was all I could say.

Kade put liquid in the bowl, and started to run the hot water in silence. I looked at him, coughed, turned to find the remote for the sound system to change the CD to Rag'n'Bone Man. I grabbed a tea towel and dried while Kade washed in silence.

It didn't take long to tidy the kitchen. When we'd finished, Kade said he had to go. I thanked him and watched him walk to the back door.

He turned as he reached it; I was right behind him. He turned and rested his hand on my cheek, then leaned in and kissed me on the lips. I felt his tongue invade my mouth and his teeth nibble at my lips before he stepped back. "I'll check on you tomorrow, Molly. Don't be dragged into whatever Alex and his father are into. I don't want to see you get hurt. Please lock the doors behind me."

With that he left just like Alexander by softly closing the door.

"Oh my God! I've only been here a day. Who the hell are these guys?"

After letting my pets out in the garden, I closed the door and locked it as instructed and put out the lights. The country air, red wine and the confusing company I was keeping had tired me out.

SIX

I was up bright and early the next morning, showered and dressed in jeans, and a t-shirt. The animals were fed and watered. I unpacked the rest of my things, then decided I was hungry. Popping in some toast, I found the keys to the garden shed and retrieved my new bike. Well, new to me. I sat in the garden munching on my breakfast as I surveyed my new prize possession.

"Well, you guys," I said to the watching dog and cat. "I think, before I go on my maiden voyage, we need to give it a bit of a clean. What do you think?" My answer was a woof and a meow. I looked over at the two animals and laughed.

Grabbing a bowl of soapy water, I started the clean-up. After an hour of elbow grease, the bike was like brand new. "Right, kids, should I give it a go before James arrives? I don't want to look a complete idiot." I looked over at them waiting for an answer, but got silence in return.

I closed the back door, took the bike by the handle bars, and steered it through the back gate to the front of the house and on to the road. Zeuss and Missy following behind. I looked both ways, there was not a soul in sight, so I threw my leg over the center bar and hopped on board. I hastily put both feet on the peddles and started off down the road. "Oh God, I'm going to fall! I'm going to fall! Come on girl you can do this." I kept muttering to myself as I wobbled along a couple of yards. I pulled the brakes and jumped off, before I fell off. I laughed. Pumped the air. Turned to Zuess and Missy shouting "Yes, I did it!" After a few more rides up and down, I felt I had it in the bag.

"Molly! Molly! I'm here." I turned around, seeing James peddling towards me, with Jacob strolling behind him. James stopped beside me, hopping off his bike. "Wow! Molly, you cleaned the bike. It looks cool."

"I've practiced, and I think I've got this. I'll lock up, then we can go for a ride. I don't think we should take Zuess and Missy until I feel more confident."

"Okie dokie, Molly."

I laughed out loud. Leaning the bike against the fence, I went to lock the doors.

The country road was quiet. James and I cycled slowly, James patiently keeping at my speed, when I knew he wanted to career ahead.

"Molly," James said. "There's a hill ahead, we go down and then up again. Will you be okay?"

I turned to make sure Jacob was still behind.

"I'm good," I said.

"Cool," he replied.

The hill was steeper than I thought it would be. I took my feet off the peddles, and free-wheeled down as did James, both of us laughing. As we reached the bottom, we both pressed on the breaks to stop as there was a lake to the left. But naturally, due to my accident-prone nature, mine didn't work.

"James! My brakes aren't working!" I looked ahead. It was either face the tree trunk in front of us or take a dip. Wet was better to my way of thinking. Taking a sharp left turn, I flew over the handle bars, somersaulted, and hit the water head first. Sinking until my bottom hit a hard surface. It was quite shallow, I stood planting my feet firmly in the mud.

"Oh my God!" I pumped the air, and started laughing. James was panicking, so I made light of the situation. He jumped off his bike. Ran into the water, jumping on me, hugging me. At first, he didn't laugh. When I hugged him, I could feel him starting to relax, and he started laughing with me. Jacob on the other hand was not amused. He came running down the hill at break-neck speed. Stopping at the edge of the water, running his hands through his hair.

"Molly! You okay? What happened?" he shouted.

"I'm fine," I laughed, wading towards dry ground. "The brakes failed."

"Did you check them before you set off?" He asked angrily.

"Well. No. I just assumed," I said.

"Never assume, you silly woman."

"Steady on, Jacob. I'm fine." I knelt and put James on his feet.

He snatched both mine and James' hands and pulled us towards the road home.

"What about the bikes?"

"I've arranged to have them collected. I'll have a look at them at the estate. Come, I need to get you both home and dry."

"But, Jacob! Its water and its summer. What's your problem?"

"You could have broken your neck. Alexander would not be happy."

"He's known me for two days. What's it to him?"

"When he takes an interest in someone, he's relentless. However, I also like you and don't want you to get hurt."

"Thank you, Jacob. I like you too." I smiled and winked at James behind Jacob's back. James just smiled, putting a hand over his mouth.

Just as we reached the top of the hill, that James and I free-wheeled down, a black SUV with blacked-out windows passed us. It turned and stopped at the water's edge. A man jumped out, opened the boot and collected both bikes.

"Wow! Jacob, that's some service you run," I laughed. My hand felt comfortable in his, like a safe feeling. James giggled, let go of Jacob's hand, then ran around to my side and grabbed mine, Jacob just grunted. The next thing, the SUV and Alexander's sports car pulled up in front of us. He jumped out and walked towards us, running his hand through his hair. Addressing Jacob, totally ignoring both James and me.

"Well, this looks very cozy. What the hell's going on, Jacob?"

"Molly's brakes failed on her bike and she took a dip. James went in to make sure she was alright. Now I'm trying to get them home to dry out," he answered.

Alexander looked at our entwined hands and turned to me. "Get in the car," he said.

"Pardon me?" I answered.

"Get in the car. You too, James. Now!"

"I will not! Who the hell do you think you are?" I turned to James. "James, you get in the car. I'll see you soon."

"Molly. Please get in the car. I'll take you home," Alexander said in a softer voice.

"No. I'll walk, thank you." I let go of Jacob's hand and stomped off, not turning around to see what was happening behind me. The next thing, I looked up to see Kade's motor bike heading towards us.

Oh great, I thought. What does he want now?

He pulled up at the side of me, taking his helmet off.

"Molly? What's going on? Why are you wet?" He looked behind me, taking in the whole scenario.

"Well, if you must know, we were free-wheeling down the hill, when my brakes failed. Instead of opting for the tree, I decided to take a dip. James came into rescue me. Jacob lost it. Alexander turned up and started shouting at me to get in his car. I lost it, told him to go to hell, and now I'm walking home." Then I started crying.

"Right. Get on my bike. I'll take you home."

"No, I don't like bikes. They scare me to death. I've only been on two bikes in my life – my dad's, he got to the end of the street before he stopped and chucked me off saying I was dangerous, and my friend Russ, who took me round the block. Said never again. He thought I was going to kill us both."

I knew I was rambling, but I couldn't help it. "Please, just go. I need to be on my own. I just met the two of you yesterday. I feel as though my life is spinning out of control, and while we're on the lay it all out there thingy, what's all this kissing about? I'm not into this kissy, touchy and feely thing. It makes me feel uncomfortable. Is something going on I don't know about. Who the hell are you people?"

With that I just stomped off again. I knew we hadn't biked far. So, my cottage should only be round the next bend in the road. I heard the bike start up again. Kade pulled up at the side of me.

"Get on the bike. I won't go fast, you'll be safe."

"No. Please go away," I said continuing to walk ahead, muttering to myself all the time that all men are bastards. I was thinking of turning gay, I so needed to talk to BFA (Best friend Alice).

SEVEN

I slammed into the house. I pulled my shoes off, threw them on the floor, and pulled my t-shirt off. Opening the washer door, I threw it in, followed by my bra, jeans, socks and panties. Standing naked, hands on my hips, I looked over at my pets, sitting on the kitchen floor, watching me.

"What?"

Zuess woofed, Missy meowed.

"Thanks guys! You don't know how lucky you are, the only issue you guys have is where your next meal comes from. I've been here two days. Two days and my life is out of control. Who the hell are these guys?"

A loud knock came from the door, followed by the handle being pushed down.

"Shit! Shit! I didn't lock the bloody door."

"Molly!" Kade stepped in. With Alexander on his heels.

"Get out! Out! Out! Out!" I yelled at the top of my voice. Kade stopped in his tracks. Alexander pushed passed him.

"Shit, Molly! I'm so sorry, we'll wait outside until you get some clothes on." They both turned, making a fast exit, just as my shoe hit the door.

"It's my house! Just so you know, you knock and wait until you're invited in," I yelled.

I ran through the living room. Up the stairs to the safety of my bedroom.

"Oh my God, how embarrassing," I muttered. I grabbed a T-shirt and some shorts, then sat on the bed taking deep breaths. After five minutes. I felt I had my anger under control.

"Right! Let's see what these idiots want," I said out loud. I made my way down the stairs to the back door. They were both sitting at the garden table talking. I opened the door hesitantly.

"What do you want?" I said angrily.

"Why would you take your clothes off, without locking the door?" Alexander asked. "Anyone could have walked in."

"They did," I snapped.

"I meant someone that you didn't know, that wanted to hurt you."

"I don't know either of you. You both landed on my door step two days ago. Everywhere I go, the two of you turn up, it's like you have a tracking device on me. What am I to you?"

Kade answered before Alexander could butt in.

"Your grandmother asked us to look out for you. Which is what we're trying to do."

"Why? I'm an accountant from the northwest, with her dog. Why would anyone try to hurt me? I've no enemies. The most danger I've ever been in is crossing the road."

"We're not saying someone is trying to hurt you, we're just keeping our promise to your grandmother," Alexander answered.

"Well, you're suffocating me. Back off."

"Well, lock the doors before getting undressed."

"I don't normally get undressed in the kitchen. I was wet and didn't want to trail the wet and dirt through the house. I don't even know why I'm explaining myself to you both. Please go. I don't want to see either of you right now."

With that, I stood up, and went into the house making a point of locking the door behind me.

EIGHT

The next few days were uneventful. I never saw sight, nor sound, of James, Alexander, or Kade. I very happily busied myself getting to know my new surroundings. Tending the gardens and general household chores. I baked, and sold a few of my creations, through a sign I'd artfully crafted and attached to the gate post.

I had now been here over a week. My bike had appeared in full working order at my back door, I assumed curtesy of Jacob. I'd ridden to the local shop and back, collecting a few supplies, but other than that I hadn't ventured very far. Zuess and Missy were inseparable, becoming fast friends. Which reminded me, I should try to ring Alice. Grabbing my phone, I scrolled through my contacts.

"Hey, Alice! What you up too?" I said cheerfully.

"Molly, how are you settling in?" she asked. "How's the hot trio?"

"Ha, ha, very funny, Alice. If you must know, I haven't seen anyone for three days. I think they took me at my word."

"Either that or the sight of you naked frightened them off," she laughed.

"You're so full of it. Are you practicing being a stand-up comic?"

"Sorry, only joking. What have you been up to?"

"Cooking and baking. Hey, and I sold some. I put up a sign on the gate, and I asked the guy at the local shop, would he be interested in taking some off me. I told him he could put a mark up on them for his trouble. I've some veg ready in the green house, so I've been selling them as well, and I've even sold a couple of sketches. So, I'm good, I feel like I've been here forever, its spooky. Oh, Alice, you'd love this place. When are you coming to visit?"

"Sorry, Molly, it's going to have to be in the next school holidays."

"That's okay, no problem, just let me know. Oh, I bike everywhere now, so I'm keeping fit. No laughing, you know how I hate exercise." I could hear her stifling a chuckle. "Okay, I'll let you go, its lovely and sunny here. I'm going to get a G & T and do a bit of sketching in the garden, then watch some TV. Love you, speak soon."

"Bye! Love you too."

I turned my surround sound up, set up on the table outside, and started sketching. As always, time slipped away, and before I knew it, the sun had gone down. As I packed everything away, my animals did their business, then wandered to sit at their bowls, looking at me expectantly.

NINE

Another sunny day, I pondered as I lay in bed. Zuess poked his head over the side of the bed and woofed. "I take it you want breakfast."

I stroked his head, then climbed out of bed. "Where is Missy?" Just then, Missy popped her head around the bedroom door and meowed.

"Okay, guys, give me a minute, I need a shower." I chuckled as I made my way to the bathroom. Fifteen minutes later, I was dressed and heading to the kitchen. "Right, guys, walkies today. I need to stock up on some things, so we'll call at the village shop." I opened the back door. My animals filed out, leaving me to prepare breakfast.

An hour later, we were trooping down the road. I swear Missy looked like she was on a modelling platform as she chasséd down the lane. I just chuckled, and shook my head, watching them both leading the way, as if they knew exactly where we were going.

I heard a large car coming up behind me, so I herded them both to the side of the road to let it pass. Instead it slowed, keeping pace with me. I looked over to see who was driving, but the windows were blacked out. I felt the hairs stand up on the back of my neck. "What the hell." The next minute the car sped up and took off. I watched it disappear. I shook my head, speeding up as we approached the village shop.

After passing the time of day with Albert, he agreed to drop off my groceries, whilst collecting his next batch of cakes. That was a relief. I didn't fancy hauling my groceries all the way back to the cottage. I do tend to over spend when food shopping. I untied Zuess, heading back home. I hadn't walked far when Alexander zoomed up. What is it with men, and fast cars?

"Hi, Molly, where are you going?"

"Home."

"Want a ride?"

"What about the guys?" I gestured towards Zuess and Missy.

He turned his head to indicate the back seat.

"Well, if you don't mind. I won't say no. We had a bit of a scare on the way down." I ushered the animals into the back and climbed in the front.

"Why? Did someone threaten you? Who was it? Did you know them?" he asked angrily.

"No, nothing like that. A SUV pulled up at the side of me, and just kept pace with me for a bit, not long, but it just unnerved me."

"Did you recognize them?"

"I didn't see who was in the car because the windows were blacked out. The only people I know here are you, Kade, your father, James, and Jacob. Oh, and Albert at the shop. So, why would anyone want to threaten me in any way?"

"There are some really bad people in the world today. You should be careful, especially in the country. Did you get the license plate?"

"No, I didn't think to."

"Give me your phone," he said, holding out his hand.

"I don't have it with me."

"You're joking! You've left the house and you're on foot in the middle of nowhere, without any means of contacting someone if you happen to get in trouble?"

"I've Zuess and Missy," I said seriously.

He shook his head. "You're unbelievable."

I shrugged, turned in my seat reaching for the seatbelt. Alexander calmly reached over and took it out of my hand and clicked it closed. Zuess poked his head through the front seats, planting his wet tongue on my cheek, whilst Missy curled up in a ball, oblivious to the tension in the car.

It was a short tense drive, with Alex simmering angrily beside me.

As we pulled up at the cottage, I hurried to unclick my seat belt and reach for the door.

"Stay put," Alexander said. He got out the car, coming around and opening my door. He took hold of my hand and helped me climb out, then pulled the seat forward, letting my pets troop out to follow me into the house.

"Get your phone, Molly! I want to programme mine and Kade's numbers in so that you can contact either one of us, should you need to. Also make sure if you leave the house, you have it with you always. Is that clear?" He almost growled the last bit.

"God. If I must, but I don't see what all the fuss is about," I muttered as I entered the kitchen and retrieved my phone from the kitchen table where I'd left it.

"Where's your shopping?"

"What?" I answered.

"Where's your food shop? You said you went to the shop. I haven't seen any bags."

"Oh, Albert said he'd drop them off when he collected his next batch of cakes later today," I answered. "When can I see James?" I asked, changing the subject. "When I said I didn't want to see you or

Kade for the rest of the week, I didn't include James. Yet you've kept him away and I miss him."

"I haven't kept him away. My father took him with him on business to Italy. They'll be back tonight. We like him to get as much practice as possible on his Italian, plus he likes seeing his family."

"Why isn't he with his mum and dad?" I asked.

"It's complicated; a story for another time," he answered distractedly as he programmed my phone, sending a text to both him and Kade, so they could pick up my number.

"Do you want a drink or anything?" I asked remembering my manners.

"No, I've to go. I've a meeting in thirty minutes," he said, retrieving his keys from the table where he had put them when he grabbed my phone. "What are your plans for this afternoon?"

"Baking, then I've a sketch I'm working on. Why?"

"Would you like to go to dinner with me?"

"As a date or a friend?" I answered nervously.

"Whatever you want it to be." He stepped towards me, never taking his eyes away from mine.

"Friends would be cool, and yes that would be nice. In the weeks I've been here I haven't strayed further than the village. It would be nice to get back to civilization again, if only for an hour or two. Do I need to get dressed up or are you talking about McDonald's?" I asked with a grin.

"Whatever you feel comfortable in."

"What time?"

"Seven thirty, sharp. I hope you're not one of these women who takes all day to get ready."

"No, I take twenty minutes tops, and I'm always ready thirty minutes before I need to be. Also, I'm never late for an appointment, if that answers your question."

Stick that in your pipe and smoke it, I thought, turning to fill the kettle. I looked over my shoulder when I didn't get an answer, only to find he had disappeared.

Charming, I thought. Now where's he gone? I hurried to the front window to see his tail lights disappear in the distance.

TEN

Albert came with my groceries, collecting some of my fresh baking. It was soon time for me to get ready for my hot date/friends outing. I had to admit, I was looking forward to having food cooked for me and not having to worry about the washing up.

I didn't have a lot of clothes, as I've never been one for going out. Before I moved out here, Alice had pestered me to buy a classy green dress, that fit me to a tee, and went well with my bobbed auburn hair. The bodice was fitted to the waist, with no sleeves, the skirt was pencil to the knee, but the back had a flared pleat.

I let my hair dry naturally so that it curled, added a dusting of powder, lip gloss, and mascara; a squirt of perfume. Hold-up stockings and black court shoes with an inch heel and I was good to go.

Good, only seven, time for a glass of wine, while I waited for Alexander. I put the TV on for the guys; they enjoy the quiz shows. Not long later, I heard the purr of an expensive car, then a knock at the front door.

I opened the door, while grabbing my purse and key from the little table.

"Sei così bella, Molly," Alexander said as he stepped in through the door.

"What does that mean?"

"It means you look beautiful. Come, our table is booked for eight, and we have a bit of a drive to get there."

After he locked the door and pocketed the key, he opened the passenger door for me. He took my hand as I tried to be as dignified as possible while sliding in, he then leaned over to fasten my seat belt. As he did, I could smell his aftershave. Oh my God. He smelled so good. Before I could process my thoughts, my mouth went into action.

"You smell good," I whispered.

"So do you." His lips were inches away from mine, I thought for a minute he was going to kiss me. After what seemed ages, but could have only been seconds, he stood and closed the door gently.

While I watched him going around the front of the car to the driver's side, I shook my head trying to unfreeze my brain. Get a grip, Molly. He's handsome, sexy, and could have his pick of the most beautiful women on the planet. Why would he be remotely interested in you? And if he is, why is he? Now there was a thought; the same question could be asked of Kade. Was I missing something?

With soft music playing in the background, Alexander expertly handled the bends in the country roads in a comfortable silence.

"How did your meeting go?" I asked to break the silence.

"Not as I had hoped," he responded. "Did Albert bring your groceries?"

"Gosh, that was a subtle change of subject. Are you a politician or a business man?"

"Do you always say what you're thinking?" he laughed.

"Mostly. Alice laughs at me."

"Who's Alice?"

"Alice is my BF, best friend, and my confidant."

"I'll bear that in mind, when I need to know your secrets." He grinned, looking in his mirror, for what must have been the fifth time.

"Is there a problem?"

"Why do you ask?"

"Because you keep looking in your rear-view mirror and frowning. I people watch; your hands are also gripping the wheel." I leaned forward, looking through the side mirror to see what he was looking at.

"Are we being followed by the SUV four cars behind?" I leaned back looking over at him.

"It seems so. Is it the same SUV that you saw this morning?"

"An SUV is a SUV. I couldn't say. But if it is, I can't imagine what they could possibly want. Should we pull over and ask them what they want? Perhaps they have me confused with someone else?"

"I don't think that's wise at the moment. I'll call one of my men to take a look." With that, he dialed a number on a little box on the dash. A dialing sound came through the speakers and the music stopped.

"Cool. I want one," I smirked. He just looked at me and frowned, as though I'd just beamed in from another planet. That made me chuckle more.

"Jacob," was the abrupt answer.

"Hey, Jacob. How are you? Thanks for fixing my bike," I answered before Alexander could say a word.

"You're welcome. Why are you on Alexander's phone?"

"I'm here, Jacob. I need you to check something out for me. A black SUV, license plate, DE 11 TA."

"Do you want back up?"

"We're going to Alfredo's."

"I'm in that direction. I'll have a look." That was followed by the dialing tone.

"Well, that was short and sweet, and he never said goodbye. Are you guys mafia, because I've seen this sort of thing on TV. Should I be frightened of you? Do you carry a gun, have you got a knife strapped to your leg? Can I see it?" I tend to ramble when I get nervous.

Alexander put his hand on my knee, which made me break out in a sweat. "Molly, take a breath and calm down. We're going for a nice meal. All Jacob will do is watch the SUV to see who they are and what they're up to."

"Right, I'm okay with that. But just so that you know, I noticed you didn't answer any of my questions." I faced forward and fiddled with my purse. We turned a corner into a small town, then pulled in to a restaurant car park, which was cramped with expensive looking cars, way out of my price bracket. Alexander turned off the engine and told me to stay where I was. He jumped out and came around to the passenger side to help me out. As we stepped around the bonnet a black 4 by 4 turned in, pulled up at the side of us and rolled the window down.

"Hi, Jacob." I smiled and raised my hand.

"Molly. You look very nice." Turning to Alexander, he nodded.

"Che hai saputo?" Alexander then turned to me. "Molly, go and stand near the car while I talk to Jacob."

"But you're speaking Italian anyway. I can't understand what you're saying."

"Never mind that, do as I ask, please."

"Bye, Jacob." I stepped back towards the car, looking through the window of the restaurant to people watch.

I turned back because I sensed someone watching me. Alexander had his back to me, but Jacob was watching while still listening to what Alexander was saying.

I turned back towards the window just in time to see Kade, a beautiful blonde and a middle-aged man being seated at a table near the window close to me.

I then heard Jacob reverse, turn, and head out of the car park and felt Alexander's hand touching my lower back.

"Are you ready, Molly? Our table should be ready."

I nodded and let him guide me to the door. I don't know why I didn't mention that I'd seen Kade. It just kind of slipped my mind, because the heat of his hand on my back was making my whole body tingle.

We were greeted by the owner who obviously knew Alexander by sight. They shook hands then he turned, heading towards a booth on the far wall. However, we had to pass Kade's table on the way. I kept my eyes on the booth ahead, but I felt Alexander's hand move from my lower back to around my waist as Kade's voice came from behind us. He had stood and moved into the aisle.

"Alexander. Molly, you look, well, you look different." He leaned in, kissing my cheek.

"Well, thank you. I think."

Alexander looked from me, to Kade before answering. "I thought you were out of town Kade?"

"I was. I just got back. I've some business to sort out, then I'm heading back home. I didn't expect to bump into you here, and with Molly."

"Were on a date," he answered with a grin.

I looked at him with a frown but remained silent. I didn't want to cause a scene, as Kade's guests were looking at us with interest. Kade didn't seem to want to introduce us. Alexander must have had the same thought, as I felt his grip on my waist tighten and he pushed me in the direction of our table. Kade took his seat again but kept discreetly looking in our direction.

"Why did you say we were on a date?" I asked as Alexander took the seat next to me. Resting his arm around the back of my chair, he began stroking the nape of my neck under my hair.

"Because I am. You came as a friend. I never said what I came as." With that he flipped open the menu with his other hand. "Would you like me to order for you?"

"No, I can order for myself, thank you." I grabbed the menu and opened it. I perused it for a full five seconds, then bit my lip. "It's in Italian. You knew it was, that's why you asked isn't it?"

With that he laughed out loud removed his hand from my neck, and grabbed my hand kissing it slowly. "You are so independent. You need to relax and just enjoy."

"Okay, translate for me and then I can make a decision." In the end, I ordered chicken livers and meatballs, with a side order of salad. Alexander did the manly thing and ordered steak and soup to start.

The conversation was light and very general. Alexander was witty and attentive, he ordered a very expensive bottle of red, of which he only had one glass, which he sipped but never seemed to go empty, yet mine did, so he kept topping me up.

Every now and again I glanced over to Kade's table, only to find him looking straight at me. After what seemed like hours, Alexander asked if I'd like a sweet or coffee. When I answered "no", he asked for the bill. As the waiter left, Kade appeared at the table.

"I'm leaving, however, I'd like to get together tomorrow to discuss something with you. Are you around?" This was directed at Alexander.

"Yes, where would you like to meet?"

"Your place is fine. Goodnight, Molly. I hoped you enjoyed your date?" Without waiting for an answer, he turned and left.

I turned to Alexander. "You've upset him because you inferred that we were dating, and we're most definitely not."

"Says who?"

"I say. I don't do boyfriends. I've always looked out for myself and I'm not about to change."

"You're a beautiful woman, Molly. Why have you never married or had children?" He reached for a strand of my hair and tucked it behind my ear.

"Because I've never met the right person. No one has ever asked me out. I'm not really a people person. I tend to work, bake, read and relax in front of the TV. I like peace and quiet and my own company or that of my dog, and now I've Missy. Although, I must say I've fallen in love with James. He's fun, very grown up, he makes me laugh, and I enjoy his company."

"Should I be jealous of my nephew?"

"Yes," I answered. I stood waiting for Alexander to let me out of the booth. He stood, grabbed my hand, then put his hand on the small of my back as we left the restaurant.

As we stepped outside, Jacob's 4 by 4 turned into the car park; he pulled in next to Alexander's car.

"Did you get my text?" Jacob asked.

"Yes." He turned to me. "Molly, Jacob is going to take you home. Something's cropped up that I've to deal with."

"Oh, okay then, no problem. Well, thank you for a lovely meal. I enjoyed it very much. Although just so you know, it was not a date."

He just smirked, took my elbow and escorted me round the car to the passenger side. He helped me in, then strapped my seat belt on. Leaning in, he kissed me on the cheek. "We'll see?" he said, closing the doors.

I turned to Jacob, smiled and said. "Home, James!" then giggled. I think I'd had too much red wine. Well I knew I had, but what the hell. I didn't go out that often.

Jacob put the car in gear, looked straight ahead and drove in silence.

Another annoyed soul, I pondered. Oh well. I rested my head back against the head rest and hummed along with the music on the radio.

"Are you drunk?" Jacob asked after about fifteen minutes of silence.

"No, why?"

"You look it. How much have you had to drink?"

"Well, now that I think about it, nearly a whole bottle of red wine. But I had a really nice meal as well, so that should be okay."

"What the hell was Alexander thinking?" he muttered.

I just closed my eyes, moving from a humming noise to all out singing, as Ed Sheeran was now playing, and he was my favorite.

"Do you know I've been to see him live," I said nodding to the radio. I giggled, then hiccupped. "Oh dear, I think you're right. It must have been the cold air when I came out the restaurant."

"Right, well, we'll be home soon. Where's your key?"

"Oh my. I think Alexander put it into his pocket. It's okay, I'll sit in the garden until he comes back with it."

"You will not!" he answered leaning forward to a gadget just like Alexander's and dialed a number.

"Kade, it's Jacob. Alexander had to leave on business. I'm taking Molly home, but Alexander put her key in his pocket when he locked up. Do you have the spare key?"

"Yes, do you want me to meet you at the cottage?"

"Yes, I might need your help. I think Molly has had too much to drink," he said looking over at me.

"Fuck! I'll bloody kill him. I'll be there in five." With that the line went dead.

I rolled my head towards Jacob. "You people have terrible manners," I muttered.

We pulled up at the cottage. "Stay put," Jacob muttered angrily. He jumped out and went around to my door, lifted me out, but kept me in his arms. I raised my arms and wrapped them around his neck, leaning in to kiss him on the mouth.

"You're very sexy, you know?" I laid my head on his shoulder, closed my eyes, and hiccupped.

"You're going to have one bad head in the morning," he chuckled.

The next minute I felt a soft pillow under my head. I tried opening my eyes but that was a mistake, because the room started spinning. I could hear two voices having a heated discussion.

"Molly, I'm going to take your dress off. I think you'll be more comfortable, and you might be sick, is that okay?"

"Kade, why are you here?" I turned to the voice, but that was another mistake.

"I've a spare key. Alexander has yours, do you remember? Jacob rang me to let you in. Now can I take this pretty dress off?"

"Okay, but don't look."

"You do know, I've already seen you naked," he laughed.

"Whatever. Can I've some water before you go?"

"Don't worry, sweetheart. I'm not going anywhere."

ELEVEN

The next day came all too soon, and with it, a hangover from hell.

"Ooooh, that hurts," I said as I swung my legs out of the bed. As I stood, I realised that all I had on was my bra and panties. "Oh no."

The night started to come back in flashes, especially being in Jacob's arms and how safe I felt. Then Kade, taking my dress off. I looked over to the wardrobe and saw my green dress hanging on a hanger. I could smell bacon and toast in the air. No pets in evidence, which meant it was either Kade or Alexander. I decided a shower would sort me out.

I shuffled down the stairs, dressed in jeans and t-shirt, feeling at least fifty percent better than I did twenty minutes earlier. Entering the kitchen, I popped into a chair, muttering a morning to Kade's back.

"Good morning, sweetheart, how's your head?"

"It's been better. I guess the wine went to my head about five minutes after I left the restaurant. It always does that and it's very annoying," I said leaning my head on my hands.

"About that. Jacob was not very happy, and neither was I. Alexander was well out of order letting you drink that much, then leaving you to take care of business. Whatever it was could've waited until he had seen you home." He looked at me. "Was it a date?"

"Was what a date?" I said looking up, knowing full well what he was talking about.

"You and Alexander. Was it a date?"

"No! I told him it wasn't. It was friends having a night out. I think he said that to wind you up. Why it would, I've no idea."

"Because we're both attracted to you, and he wanted me to feel that he had the upper hand, obviously," he said, placing two pieces of toast and some bacon in front of me. "Now eat, you'll feel much better."

Kade's mobile began to ring. "Well, it's about time, you returned my call. Yes, she's fine this morning, apart from a headache. What were you thinking, leaving her with Jacob?" As I could only hear half of the conversation, and Kade had walked away from me, I lost interest and focused on my breakfast. When I looked up, Kade was in front of me again.

"I'm going to head off. What're your plans for today?"

"I'm going to take Zuess for a walk, to clear my head, then potter. Why?"

"Just asking. Are you okay?"

"Yes, Kade. I'm twenty-eight years old and have had a hangover before. I've survived just fine on my own up to now. Shouldn't you be at work anyway?"

"I'm free-lance."

"Free-lance, at what exactly?"

"If I told you that, I'd have to kill you. I mentioned that before." He laughed and planted a kiss on my cheek, then left.

I looked at my two pets. "Interesting guys. Very interesting. I'm missing something here, but mark my words. I'll get to the bottom of it."

TWELVE

I went in search of my shoes. "Time for a walk guys." They raised their heads from the sofa but didn't move. "I take it that's a no then?" Their heads went down and their eyes closed. "Lazy pair," I muttered.

Michael Bublé was singing from the kitchen, so I turned in search of my mobile. Expecting it to be Alice, I was surprised to see a private number displayed.

"Hello, Molly speaking," I answered.

"Molly, dear, it's James' grandfather. How are you today?"

"You heard about last night then? Are there no secrets?"

"No. What happened last night, dear? Are you hurt?" he asked in a concerned fatherly voice.

"No, never mind. What can I do for you?"

"I was wondering if you might do me a big favor. James' nanny has been called home unexpectedly, a family crisis, which means James is bored and is left to his own devices. I wondered if you'd spend time with him, until his nanny returns?" Silence followed. "I'd of course pay you for your time."

"That's not necessary. I'd love to spend time with James. Are you sending him over?"

"I'd prefer it if you'd come here. You can of course bring your pets, if you so wish."

"Yes, of course. When would you like me to come?"

"Well, there's no time like the present. Would you like Jacob to come for you?"

"Thank you, but no. You're only next door. I'm sure I can find my way on my own." The last thing I needed was to bump into Jacob after last night. I vaguely remember the word "sexy" falling out of my loose drunken lips. "I'll grab some things and be there in around fifteen minutes. Does that work for you?"

"Yes, dear, that will be perfect. I'll tell security to expect you. And, Molly, thank you so much. I love my grandson. When he's unhappy, I'm unhappy too."

"Um, one thing before you go. Does Alexander know about this?"

"No, I don't run everything by my son. I'm the head of this family."

"Err, right, no problem, see you soon then." I pressed end and frowned at my phone. Oh my, what was I doing? I thought. On the plus side, I could do some investigating and see what secrets lie behind the grey wall.

Gathering some sketch pads, pencils, and paints, I locked the doors and made my way to my neighbors.

I approached the iron gates and peered through, raising my hand to get the attention of the man in the black suit and tie. Oh my God, it's like bloody Fort Knox. I wonder what the hell they're into that requires this kind of security.

"You must be Molly. I'm expecting you. I need to check your bag and do a body search before I can let you through to the main house, if that's okay?"

"No! Why would you want to search me?"

"Well, I'm sorry, Miss, but I'll get in serious trouble with my boss if I let you through without a search. What if you're concealing a weapon or a bomb?"

"Are you serious? I've come to play with James and was asked to do so by his grandfather. Why the hell would you think I was here to kill anyone? Is Jacob or Alexander here? I'll speak to them."

"Alexander's out on business. Jacob's coming across the lawn behind you. He must have spotted our misunderstanding on the house camera. I'm really sorry, Miss Molly, I'm only following orders. I've to search everyone, no exceptions, I was told."

"What's your name?" I asked.

"Ed, Miss."

"Okay, Ed. Leave me to do the talking. It's not your fault that I didn't agree to the search. It's not as though this is a government building or anything. The whole thing is just bizarre."

"Molly!" Jacob growled as he approached me. "What's the problem? Life is never dull around you."

"Well, I was asked to come over and keep James company, however Ed here won't let me in without doing a body search or checking my bag, and I'm refusing to let him. So, I think I'll just wander back to my cottage and get back to my pottering." I turned, heading back to the gate.

"You're being unreasonable. You do know that, don't you? Ed here has a job to do with no exceptions. Why can't you just let him do what he's supposed to do?"

"I'm not letting some strange man, who could in fact be a pervert, run his hands all over my body." I said it with as much outrage as I could muster, trying not to look at Ed. He had his head down and looked as though he'd like to be anywhere else but here.

"Well, they do it at the airport. I'm sure you've never kicked up such a stink there."

"Well, I wouldn't know, now would I? I've never been to the airport or on a plane." This was a down-right lie but how was he to know? "And seeing as this isn't a government building, I'm exercising my civil rights."

"For God's sake, Molly! You're being so unreasonable. Will you let me do it then?"

"No! Go to hell." I said, turning then grabbing at the gate to escape.

"Oh no you don't!" With that he swung me round, lifting both my arms up over my head. He quickly ran his hands down both arms, over the front of my body, between my breasts, then down my back and both my legs. Lastly, he ran his hands over my bottom and over my lady parts in the front. He then snatched up my bag from where it had fallen on the ground, looked through it, then threw it back at me. I just about caught it and seized it against my chest. I've never been so embarrassed in my life. Well maybe I have, however I'd not go into that right now.

"That took two seconds. Instead you had to make a song-and-dance about it. Come on, I'll take you to James. He's no idea you're coming and it will make his day." With that, he grabbed my hand and dragged me behind him.

Speaking to Jacob's back, I asked, "Why on earth would you have to search all visitors? Why is security on the gate? Are you mafia? You do come from Italy after all. I asked Alexander and he avoided the question. Do you carry a gun? Or a knife down your sock like in the movies?"

"Do you always get verbal diarrhea when you're nervous?"

"I'm not nervous. I just need to know whether there's a risk that I could pop my clogs before dinner because one of your rivals wants to get their hands on this little empire in the middle of nowhere. I've an invested interest in staying alive until tomorrow, as I've to make another batch of cakes for Albert."

I'd never heard Jacob laugh before, but he was obviously amused about something I'd said. Just then, we rounded a corner and James came hurtling towards me, wrapping his arms around my waist, giving me a hug.

"Molly! Molly! You came to see me. Can you stay?"

"Yes, James. I thought we could do some painting and you could show me around. What do you think?"

"Cool!" He smiled up at me and my heart melted.

James was as good as his word. I was whisked around the most beautiful house on the planet. It was a mixture of modern and old, each room having its own uniqueness. The whole house was breathtaking.

Jacob had disappeared, and the only person we'd bumped into was the house keeper. She was a lovely woman called Maria, who obviously was besotted by James, which made me feel better.

The house was like a fortress. I was sure it must feel a bit like a prison for a young boy. Maria had said she'd bring lunch out in an hour, so we had decided to have a game of badminton before we ate, leaving the afternoon free for painting and drawing.

"James, are you going to give me a chance to win a game?" I shouted from the grass where I'd landed for the umpteenth time on my butt.

"My grandfather said you should always play to win. Always."

"Well, I think it's the taking part and having fun that matters. Winning's just a bonus."

"I'll tell him that. Perhaps he'll not be so grumpy when I outmaneuver him in chess."

"I'm sure he'll love my input." I laughed out loud while picturing the old man's frown in my head.

I was saved then by the arrival of Maria with our lunch. She was holding a picnic basket and a blanket under her arm. I jumped up and went to give her a hand.

"Maria, you shouldn't have gone to all this trouble."

"The boy should enjoy the experience of a picnic; do you not agree?" she asked smiling.

I looked into her eyes, smiling as well. "Of course. Will you join us? I'm sure you're allowed a break."

"Why not? I will, if you don't mind. You look like you're having so much fun."

The food was delicious, as I knew it would be, Maria and James were animated in their recounts of James's attempts to escape the strict rules of the house behind the wall. It was a beautiful afternoon and so peaceful. Looking over at James, my laughter died on my lips as I noticed a bright red spot of light, moving slowly across his chest. Maria followed my eyes and gasped behind her hand.

"Maria, take some of the plates into the house as though you're starting to clear away, and get Jacob."

I turned to James and crawled to him on my hands and knees, blocking his body with mine. "James, how about we play hide and seek? I'll close my eyes and count to ten, and you go and hide in the house as fast as you can. You'll have to be fast though because I'll only give you to the count of ten, then I'm coming, ready or not. Starting now – one, two, three."

I peeked through my closed eyes to see him disappearing into the house. Maria had also done as I'd asked. I finished my counting. "Coming, ready or not." I jumped up and ran to the house, diving through the patio door, slamming it shut as I went. I turned, only to come up against a solid wall of muscle. Two arms grabbed me and pulled me out of the view of the window.

"Shit, Jacob! You nearly gave me a heart attack."

"Molly, are you okay? Where's James?"

"I sent him to hide in the house. I said it was a game. I saw a red spot moving across his chest. I've seen enough Strikeback episodes to realise a sniper lining up a shot."

"Really?" He asked, raising an eyebrow.

"Shouldn't you be out there looking for whoever it was?" I could feel my temper rising and I'm sure he thought I was missing a few marbles.

"I sent my men to check the grounds, but if it was someone trying to hurt James, he'd already be dead. The shot was there to take. It was obviously only meant as a warning."

I shook off his hands that were still holding me in front of him. "What the hell is going on? Why would anyone try to harm an eight-year-old boy? And why would his family put him in that kind of danger?"

"These are questions I can't answer. You'll have to ask Alexander."

"Right! Where is he?"

"Out, but he's on his way back."

With that, I stepped around him, muttering, and went in search of James.

"James, James, where are you?" I looked behind settees, in cupboards, and even in the kitchen pantry. After about thirty minutes I gave up.

"Maria, do you know where he is?" I asked smiling. She indicated with her head to the wet room.

I crept to the door and popped my head round. All I could see was a pair of little legs and feet sticking out from under the coats. I tiptoed forward, grabbing him around the waist, lifting him up and swinging him round. "Found you." He laughed and wrapped his legs around me giggling.

Just then I heard the arrival of a powerful car, marking Alexander's return. We shuffled through to the kitchen, James still in my arms. I heard raised voices coming from the hallway, so we headed in that direction.

Alexander was having a heated argument with Jacob, who was giving as much as he got. However, it was the woman that stood behind them that took my interest. She was stunning and was obviously from money. Blonde, wearing expensive clothes and shoes. She gave a gentle cough alerting Alexander and Jacob to our presence.

"James, how nice to see you again." The blonde stepped towards us. I felt James stiffen in my arms and his arms tighten around my neck.

"And who is this, have you a new nanny?" the blonde asked.

"No!" Alexander and Jacob said together.

I released one of my hands, holding it out to her. "Molly. I'm James's friend and a neighbor. So nice to meet you. And you are?"

"A business associate of the family. Aren't you a bit old for James? Or do you have your sights on someone else?" I stepped back as though I'd been slapped. Gosh, that's a woman with a lot of issues.

"Right, well, I think I'll head back home now that you're back, Alexander." I disentangled James, planting him on his feet.

"Oh, Molly, please stay," James said, grabbing my hand.

"I've to go, sport. I've some things to do, but I'll come back tomorrow and we'll draw some more, is that okay?" That got a snort from the blonde. "Sorry, didn't catch your name?" I said.

"I didn't give it," she said, dismissing me. She then turned towards Alexander, putting her hand on his arm. "Darling, we need to make that call."

"Molly, Jacob will take you home."

"That's not necessary, I'll walk."

Jacob intervened by grabbing my arm and gently leading me away from the couple.

"Well, that was interesting," I said as we stepped through the front door. "Are they an item? What's with her refusing to tell me her name?"

"I've no idea. It's not my place to know."

"That's total bollocks and you know it. You know everything and more, you just don't want to tell me."

"Come on, I'll walk you back."

"No, thank you, I can manage. I'm sure you've things to do." With that I turned and walked down the long drive towards the gate I'd come through earlier. I turned at the end of the drive to find Jacob still watching me, hands in his pockets. I turned toward the gatehouse where Ed was still at his post. I went to the gate and pulled as Ed released the lock to let me out.

The rest of the day went without incident. Night fell as we, meaning me and my pets, settled down to watch some TV and chill.

My mobile rang some time later; I didn't recognize the number.

"Molly speaking." There was silence on the other end. "Hello? Hello?" Nothing, then the dialing tone. I clicked the phone off and tossed it on the cushion. "I'm beginning to think this move was not a good idea, Zeussy. Something's not quite right."

THIRTEEN

The next day brought a change in the weather. The rain was coming down in torrents and the animals refused to go out to use the bathroom. I left the door ajar in case they got desperate, then started making my next batch of cakes for Albert to collect later. I turned the music center on loud with my favorite tunes on shuffle. Occasionally, I stopped what I was doing to concentrate on the music. I was sure I could hear humming again, however as soon as I stopped to listen, it died away. I was lost in thought, when a voice made me jump.

"Molly, can I come in?" Kade popped his head around the door.

"Hi, Kade, yes come in."

"I missed you yesterday. I knocked but you didn't answer, yet your car was on the drive."

"I was invited to visit with James by his grandfather. I met a friend of Alexander's, a woman friend. Blonde, tall, well-dressed, had a bit of an attitude. Introduced herself as a business associate, but no name. She called him 'darlin' a couple of times and kept grabbing his arm. Do you know who she was, his girlfriend perhaps?"

"No, sorry. As far as I'm aware, he isn't involved with anyone. Why? Are you interested in him?"

"No," I said with a frown. "Just worried about James. He didn't seem to like her very much."

I didn't mention the red dot scenario. I didn't think Jacob would be very happy if I started blabbing about the incident. Everything seemed to be on a need-to-know basis behind the wall and I didn't fancy being dead. These people were certainly very intimidating, not a family to mess with.

"Good. Because I'd like to take you to dinner tomorrow night. And I promise I'll bring you home at the end of the evening. Seeing as I don't have a head of security to do it."

"Okay. Yes, that would be nice." I smiled at him and blushed. Oh my, I thought, this is going to get a bit messy. I've gone from getting zero attention from the opposite sex to being surrounded by testosterone. Nice, but scary.

"No bike though," I stated.

"No bike? That's no problem, I've a car," he laughed. "I'll pick you up at seven."

"I can't wait. See you tomorrow."

He then nodded at me and left.

Oh my God, I thought. What am I going to wear? I can't wear the same green dress as last time. I'd never been one for going out, so my evening wear was a bit limited. Perhaps I should have a ride to the nearest town and see if I can pick something up. But first, I needed to find out if James needed me. I picked up my mobile. I went through the address list to find the number Alexander had saved there.

The phone rang several times before it was picked up. "Molly, do you have a problem?"

"Hello, Alexander. No, I was only wondering if you needed me to watch James today?"

"No, that will not be necessary. He's gone with his grandfather for the day. In light of what happened yesterday, we thought it would be best to get him off the estate while we investigate who was on the grounds and how they breached our security."

"Right, well, that leaves my day free then. I wanted to go into the nearest sizable town for some things. Can you suggest the best place to go? I haven't been further than the Glenwillow village shop on my own."

"That would be Blackwater, but it depends what you're looking to pick up. There's a large supermarket and some clothing outlets. However, I'm not sure I like the idea of you going off alone. We've yet to establish who's tailing you in the SUV."

"I'm sure it's nothing. I've nothing of value and I don't have any enemies. I'll be fine. How long would it take a thirty-mile-an-hour driver in her little bubble machine to get there?" I laughed.

"Around an hour. I'll send Jacob over, he can take you," he said, without a hint of humor.

"No, don't be silly, that's absolutely not necessary. I'm twenty-eight years old, I don't need a baby sitter. Thank you for the information. I'll see you soon."

With that, I broke the connection, grabbed my keys and my bag, then dived for the door, knowing full well that by now Alexander would be searching for Jacob to send him over. That was so not going to happen.

I decided I didn't have time to program Tim, my charming sat-navigator. No problem, I thought. I'd follow the signs and do it the old-fashioned way. It would be an adventure. If I got lost, well I'd all day, so no problem. I could always turn around. Little did I know…

Thirty minutes later, following the signs, and singing away to my tunes down the country lanes, something caught my eye in the rear-view mirror.

It was quite a way back, and the roads were winding, so I only caught a glimpse as I turned the next bend. A black SUV.

I slowed down. I was just being paranoid. Perhaps it was Jacob following me or some random person. It couldn't possibly be the same SUV that scared me to death yesterday. Perhaps it wasn't the best idea to slow down. I never was the one with the greatest common sense.

The next thing I knew, the black SUV came speeding up behind and sat on my bumper. Shit, this isn't going to end well. I began to speed up, as did the SUV.

Unfortunately, my little Beetle couldn't match its speed. The next thing I knew I was jolted forward, as the SUV rammed into the back of my car.

I pressed my foot on the accelerator and my car slowly climbed to its top speed. I swerved around the next corner, nearly losing control, when the SUV hit me again.

"Oh my God, I'm going to die"" I hadn't a clue who I was telling, but I felt I needed to let someone on the other side know I was coming as a gate crasher.

As the SUV hit me a third time, my tire hit a large stone on the side of the road, putting the car into a spin. The car continued to move forward, sliding towards the biggest majestic oak I've ever seen. I curled into the smallest ball I could manage while still having my seat belt on.

There was an incredibly loud crunching sound of metal as the side of my car hit the tree. My head banged against something hard and all I could see for several seconds were bright lights and black dots.

From my haze of pain, I could make out the SUV pulling to my side. All I could think to do was to close my eyes and slump forward. Maybe if they thought they'd already killed me, they'd stop trying.

It must have worked. After a moment, I heard its engine rev then speed off. I let out a breath then surrendered to the darkness that claimed me.

~~~~

I don't know how long I was out. Through a fog, I could hear someone calling my name.

"Molly? Molly, sweetheart, wake up. I need you to push the door so I can get you out." I knew the voice, but was struggling to open my eyes. I shook my head trying my best to respond but it felt so peaceful in this place. It was so calm and tranquil.

"Go away," I mumbled. "I'm so sleepy. Wake me up later."

"Molly, its Jacob. Sweetheart, can you open your eyes for me. You've had an accident and you're hurt. I need you to open the lock on the door so I can get you out. Do you understand? Come on, look at me, Molly. Open your eyes."

The fog started to clear in my brain. What's Jacob doing here? I opened one eye, then the other, and peered through the cracked window. Then the memories started to come back to me. I started shaking and tears started to cascade down my cheeks.

"Jacob? Jacob, get me out of here. I don't want to die." I was sobbing now and shaking so hard my teeth were chattering.

"Molly, listen to me, you're going into shock. I need you to breathe nice and slow until you calm down, then I need you to pull the latch on the door handle to unlock the door so I can pull you out. Now, in your own time, slow your breathing down. Come on, you can do this."

I looked into his eyes and his calm face, then felt myself slowly taking some control back. His eyes never left mine as he coaxed me out of my panic. I slowly reached for the door handle and pulled, releasing the lock.

"Good girl," he said as he pulled the door open and leaned in. "Now, Molly, I need you to keep perfectly still while I check to see what the damage is, then I'll help you out. Okay, sweetheart?" I just nodded, as fresh tears fell down my cheeks.

He cupped the side of my face with his hand. "Are you hurting anywhere in particular?" I shook my head instead of answering.

"Okay, that's good. I'm going to run my hands down your legs, arms, and back. Right, now I want you to tell me if you have any sharp pains or feel uncomfortable. Can you do that for me?"

I nodded again and sniffed. He very gently ran his hands through my hair, around my neck, worked his way down each of my arms, then each of my legs.

"Anything?" he asked. I shook my head again.

"Now, gently lean forward so I can check your spine." I did as he asked.

"Anything?" I shook my head again.

"Okay, sweetheart, good. I'm going to get this seatbelt off you, then I'm going to lift you out." He leaned over me and pressed the release. Nothing happened. He pressed again, nothing. "Shit, it's jammed."

He reached down his leg, lifting his jeans to retrieve a knife that was in an ankle strap, then he raised his eyes to mine.

"I won't ask why you have a knife strapped to your leg because its none of my business," I said, raising an eyebrow. "But are you sure you're not mafia?"

He ignored my question, slicing through the seatbelt, and lifting me into his arms. He stepped back from the train wreck that was my car.

As he lifted me, I realised I enjoyed being in his arms, even under the horrible circumstances. He was wearing some sort of cologne and it added to his overall sexiness.

Kade's bike came to a stop beside us. The deep rumble of the motorcycle abruptly stopped as he shut down the big machine.

Pulling his helmet off, he ran towards us, with a scowl on his face. "What the fuck happened now?" He turned and shouted to me. "You're a bloody magnet for trouble."

Jacob answered. "Someone forced her off the road. Black SUV. I saw it speed off as I came around the corner. No license plate that I could see."

"But what about my car? Can it be repaired?"

They both looked at me with raised eyebrows. "Never mind the bloody car," Jacob muttered. "We need to get you to the hospital and have you checked out."

"I don't need to go to the hospital, I'm okay, just a bit shaken, that's all."

"You're going to the hospital, end of discussion. Kade, open the car door."

"No. I'm not! Now put me down, please."

"Kade, door, now," Jacob said through gritted teeth. "God, Molly. You're one stubborn woman."

"No, I'm not. I just don't see the point of wasting four hours in A and E when I know I'm fine."

"But, Molly, you passed out. For a good five minutes. You could have a concussion." The veins in his neck were growing at an alarming rate.

"You need to take a chill pill, Jacob. You're going to have blood pressure problems in the future, I can feel it in my water." I patted him on the shoulder.

"Well, if I do, I'll make sure to tell the doctor I only started having problems about a month ago."

"Really? What happened a month ago?"

"You!" They both replied together.

"Oh… That's so rude. Now can you put me down so I can ring someone to tow my car and give me a ride home? I'm obviously not going shopping now."

Not releasing me from his hold, Jacob spoke in a determined tone. "I'll sort out your car and get you home. Kade, can you please open the car door while I strap her in and gag her, before I throttle her?"

"You're such a gentleman," I grumbled in his ear.

Kade opened the passenger side door and Jacob gently put me down. He strapped the belt around me and covered me with his jacket.

He closed the door, stepping back to talk with Kade. After a brief discussion, they both conversed on their mobiles. I was left to ponder what had just happened and why someone was so desperate to send me to the ever after.

After about twenty minutes, the driver's door opened. "Molly, don't go to sleep. Kade will wait here for the tow truck while I take you home." I just nodded, then looked forward, trying to stay awake.

Ten minutes of silence followed while Jacob started to drive me home. As my thoughts started to come together, I turned and looked at him. "Why is this happening?"

"I'm sorry, Molly. I don't know, but I'm going to find out."

"I'm an out-of-work accountant, I've no enemies, I'm new to this part of the country, I've never parked on a double yellow line, never mind ever broke the law. Why would someone want me wrapped around a tree? The only thing exciting that's ever happened to me is being left a beautiful cottage by a grandmother I never even knew. Maybe that's it? Maybe someone thinks that they should've inherited the cottage instead of me?"

"What about ex's?"

"Pardon?"

"Ex-boyfriends." He looked at me with raised eyebrows.

"Oh, I haven't got any."

"You mean you've never had a relationship?"

"No, I mean I've never had a serious boyfriend. I've been on dates, but no one's ever rocked my boat, so I've never taken it any further."

"God, Molly, how old are you, maybe twenty-eight? And you've never had a boyfriend?" He sounded angry.

"No, why would I lie?"

"I believe you. I just find it incredible, and a little sad."

"Why? Not everybody's motivated by sex."

"Who mentioned sex? Definitely not me."

"You're a man. They're ruled by their middle leg."

With that he started laughing. It was a beautiful sound. It was good hearing him let go of the iron control of his emotions. He pulled up at my cottage and turned the engine off.

"Stay there, please," he said as he climbed out and went around to open my door.

He reached in and easily lifted me out of the car. I could again smell his cologne. "Hey," I said. "I can walk."

"I didn't say you couldn't. I was just going to help you out of the car. He put me on my feet and held his hand out. "Keys, please?"

"Right, that's okay then. I handed him the keys. He put his hand at the base of my spine and gently pushed me forward towards the front door.

"You don't have to see me in. I'll be alright from here."

"I want to check you over properly, as you won't go and get checked out at the hospital."

"Jacob, that's really not necessary. I'll be fine. I need to get in touch with my insurance and sort things out. I'll need to get my car fixed and back as soon as possible."

"Get me the details and I'll sort it out for you."

"Really, you don't have to do that. I've looked after myself since I was a teenager. I'm quite capable of handling the car insurance."

"Look, will you please sit down? I want to look you over. I'll sort this out for you. Stop being so stubborn, woman."

I let out a sigh and sat down on the sofa.

"Good girl. Now do you want a cup of tea?" he said, moving to the kitchen.

"Okay, black, no sugar. I'm sweet enough." God, I didn't just say that did I? He turned and frowned, so I frowned back.

After I was settled with my tea, he sat down. "Right, take your t-shirt off?"

"Pardon?"

"I said remove your t-shirt. I want to check for bruising."

"No way. You have absolutely no chance."

"Just how old are you again? You've been to the beach, right? Or the swimming baths? Have you something I haven't seen on a woman before?"

"No, but you haven't seen mine and you're not going to."

"You're absolutely unbelievable. Get a grip and grow up."

"No, I can check myself, thank you very much." I put my head down and stared into my tea cup. I looked over at Zeuss and Missy who were wrapped around one another, staring at me from the arm chair. God, a lot of help they were.

"Right, get me your car details then and I'll sort that out."

"Well, that will take some finding. They're in one of the boxes I haven't unpacked yet."

"Bloody hell, Molly! Is anything ever simple in your life?"

"Well, it was until I moved down here," I bounced back at him.

70

"Where's the box of papers?"

I could hear Jacob rooting around in the spare room. I remember thinking, I'd close my eyes and have a minute.

"Molly, wake up. The doctor's on his way to have a look at you."

"I wasn't asleep. I was resting my eyes."

"Is that why you were snoring?"

"I don't snore!"

"Yes, you do."

"I don't."

With that, Zuess let out a low woof. "See, even your dog agrees."

"You're so not funny. What doctor? I don't have a doctor."

"Antonio asked his doctor to check you out."

"Who's Antonio?"

"Alexander's father."

"Oh, that's nice of him. So, his name's Antonio." I said raising my eyebrows.

"Yes," he looked up from the papers he was reading. "Right. I'll sort this insurance out before the doctor arrives. If he says everything's okay and you don't have to go to the hospital, Antonio wants to have a talk with you up at the house."

"What about?"

He just shrugged and started dialing on his mobile. "Good afternoon. I'd like to report an accident. My fiancée…"

I nearly choked as the mouthful of tea I'd just sipped made a reappearance out of my mouth. "Fiancée?" I mouthed at him.

He stood, turned his back, and walked into the kitchen. Just then there was a knock at the front door. I gingerly got to my feet and shuffled to answer it.

"Molly? I'm Doctor Sinclair. Antonio asked that I call. It appears you've had a bit of a bump in your car?"

I opened the door wider. "Yes, thank you for calling, Doctor. It was very nice of you to make a house visit." I waved him through to the living room.

"Now, young lady, let's have a look at you," he said with a warm smile. Just then Jacob made a reappearance, obviously finished with the insurance company.

"Ah! Jacob nice to see you again." The good doctor shook Jacob's hand with familiarity, while Jacob just nodded. Before I could get a word out Jacob butted in.

"Molly lost control of her car and hit a tree. She's too stubborn to go the hospital. When I found her, she was unconscious and the seat belt had jammed. She must have a lot of bruising to her upper body."

The doctor, who was in his late fifties, turned to me. "Right then, Molly, let's have a look at you, take a seat."

I looked from the doctor to Jacob, then sat down with a sigh. The doctor checked my eyes with a light, ran his hands over my scalp, around my neck, my legs, and my arms, before turning to Jacob.

"Do you want to wait in the kitchen for a moment?" Jacob just nodded and left the room.

After checking out my chest and ribs, Dr. Sinclair declared I'd no major injuries, although I'd have quite a lot of bruising that I could manage with paracetamol. He then left with a friendly wave and a fatherly smile.

Jacob was seeing to the animals, so I waited until he returned and sat down next to me.

"Do you want to have a soak in the bath for a bit?" he asked. "It'll ease the aches and bring out the bruising. I'll then take you over to the house to see Antonio."

I didn't answer his question. "What did the insurance say?"

"That they'd send an assessor out and let me know whether it can be repaired."

"What about letting me know?"

He smiled. "Well, as your fiancé, the operator agreed to deal with me."

I frowned. "What happened to data protection?"

"I knew your security details."

"What? How? Oh, forget it. Don't even bother answering that. I'm going for that bath, you don't have to wait for me. I'm quite capable of finding my way to the house."

"I'll wait. It's not safe for you to be alone until we find the people responsible for running you off the road." He reached over for the remote and switched on the TV.

I muttered to myself all the way up the stairs. Slamming the bathroom door, making sure the sound of the bolt locking could be heard loud and clear.

An hour later and in a better frame of mind, I switched the TV off and turned to Jacob. "Right, I'm ready."

He picked his jacket up off the arm of the chair where he had left it and held his hand out to me. "Keys?" I looked at him, raised my eyebrows, then dropped them from a height into his hand. He followed me out, locking the door behind me, then pocketing the keys.

"Keys." I said as I held my hand out.

"I'll be bringing you back, so you don't need them."

He turned to the passenger side door, opening it for me. "Get in."

FOURTEEN

This time, as we approached the gates of the estate, they opened for us. Jacob didn't stop, he just increased his speed up the drive. He stopped the car and told me to wait, as he jumped out and came around to my door. As I climbed out, he put his hand at the base of my spine, gently pushing me to the front door. As we approached, it was opened by a man I'd never seen before.

"They're in the study, Jacob," was all he said.

We crossed the wide entrance hall, making our way down a long corridor to a solid-looking door. Jacob knocked then opened the door, pushing me in. He stepped behind me, closing the door.

James' grandfather sat behind a large desk that reeked expensive and the walls were lined with bookcases filled with books. It was a very masculine room. Alexander was standing by the window.

"Come in, Molly, dear. Sit. I want to talk to you about something."

"I don't understand," I said stepping forward. Everyone else stayed where they were.

"You will, my dear. I need you not to interrupt me and when I've finished, I'll answer all your questions, is that okay?" I just nodded and sat down in the chair opposite him.

"I met Francesca many years ago, about a year or two after my first wife had died. I'd two young boys and a very demanding business.

We were both attracted to one another and our friendship gradually turned into love. I bought the cottage for Francesca, but we kept our relationship a secret. I felt if anyone knew about us, she'd become a target for my enemies, of which I've many. After we had been in a relationship for a couple of years, Francesca fell pregnant. As the day of the baby's birth came nearer, we had to make a decision that would break both of our hearts; however, it would keep our new child safe and out of harm's way. Francesca's sister and her husband wanted children but had never been blessed, so we asked her to bring our child up as her own. We both kept track of our daughter and when Francesca died, she felt it only right that the cottage, along with everything she had, be left to our daughter. You're my daughter, Molly. The reason I'm telling you this now is, I don't know who or how, but someone's found out and they're targeting you."

He sat back in his chair and looked at me in silence.

My hands were shaking, and it was only when I covered my face that I realised I was crying uncontrollably. "You're lying. You're not my father. My mother and father are dead. Why would you say those things? I don't know any of you. Why are you doing this to me? I need to leave now, please leave me alone, all of you."

I leapt out of the chair and hurried to the door, pushing Jacob out of the way. I put my hand on the handle; however, Jacob stopped me by putting his large hand on top of mine.

Behind me Antonio shouted, "Molly, I need you to move into this house so I can protect you! What I've told you is true."

"Tell me, Alexander. How long have you known? Why did you flirt with me and take me out on a date?"

"I've known since Francesca died. I took you out and flirted with you because Kade was sniffing around. He's counter intelligence and has been snooping around our business for years."

"Marvelous, bloody marvelous." I looked down at the hand on top of mine then turned to Jacob. "Get your hand off me."

He stepped back; I opened the door and just ran. Down the hall, out of the front door and down the drive until I came to the gate house, shouting to Ed to open the gate for me. I didn't stop running until I reached my front door, which was locked. Then I realised that Jacob had pocketed the key.

"Shit, shit, shit." I turned and slid to the porch then sobbed until I'd no tears left. I leaned my head back against the door and closed my eyes.

I don't know how long I'd been sitting there, when I heard a car approach and pull into the drive. I didn't move or open my eyes because I knew it would be Jacob. However, when I heard two doors slam, I jerked up, frightened that my would-be attackers had returned. I started to breathe again when my eyes met Jacob's, then turned to Alexander.

Alexander came towards me and crouched down until he was eye level. "Molly, I know you're upset. Your world and everything you thought you knew about yourself has been turned on its axis, however you're a big girl and grounded. You know it's not safe for you to live here on your own, you'll be safer at the house with us until we find out what's going on."

"No, if anything I should go back home, to my simple but boring life, with friends that love me."

"I'm afraid that's no longer an option, it doesn't matter where you go. Whoever's targeting you will find you and hurt either you or your friends. I know you wouldn't want that. Whether you believe Antonio or not, the truth is you're my sister and I'll protect you at any cost."

"I want a paternity test," I said.

"What? Don't be bloody ridiculous, you look the image of Francesca with your auburn hair, freckles and slight frame, plus you have Father's eyes."

"Well, that's it then. Everyone will know who I am and I didn't know that, would I, because I never met her, or even knew about her or him until I was left this bloody inheritance."

"I think we need to work on your gutter mouth, it's not lady-like to swear," Alexander said with a smile.

"Jacob, give me my keys so I can get in my bloody house and don't either of you pocket my keys again. Is that clear? I'm sick to death of being locked out of my own house."

Snatching the keys off Jacob, I turned, opened the door and slammed it shut before either of them could enter. Leaning back, I heard Jacob say, "Well, that went well."

I ran up the stairs, threw myself on the bed, and took deep breaths. After ten minutes of breathing in and out, trying to calm myself, I stripped off my clothes and put my pj's on. My nightwear consisted of skimpy shorts and a short t-shirt that just about covered my chest.

I was in need of a stiff drink or three, then I'd try to make some sense of the whole day, which had turned into an utter nightmare. After putting my clothes away, I made my way down the stairs to find said stiff drink. I made my way through to the kitchen, were I nearly died of a heart attack. Jacob was leaning back against the work top, gin bottle and tonic out, and a glass held out to me with ice and lemon.

"Thought you might need this."

Ignoring him. "How'd you get in?"

"Spare key."

"Where's Alexander?"

"Busy."

"Why are you here?"

"To watch out for you, and before you ask, I'm staying the night." He smiled.

"In your dreams, matey."

"Molly, someone's out there trying their hardest to hurt you. Come and live on the estate where I can look after you properly."

"No, subject closed. Did the insurance say whether I could have a hire car until mine is repaired?"

"Yes; however, I refused."

"You did what?"

"It's not safe. If you need to go anywhere, either one of my men or I will take you."

I couldn't help myself as I stomped over to him like a spoilt child, grabbed my drink, then stomped into the living room.

"I need to go shopping."

"Why? What do you need? Can't you order online for delivery?"

"No, I need something for tomorrow."

"Right, tell me what you need and I'll pick it up for you tomorrow while I'm out on business."

"No. I need a dress and I'd like to choose my own and try it on."

"And why do you need a new dress?"

"Because I'm going out to dinner."

"Oh no, you're not."

"Oh yes, I am. And no one, and I mean no one, is going to stop me."

By this time, he'd come to stand in front of me, so I stood on my tip toes and got right in his face.

"Is that clear?"

He looked straight into my eyes, lifting both his hands in what seemed slow motion, he cupped each side of my face, bringing his lips down on to mine. His lips were soft at first. However, as his kiss lengthened, he prized my lips open with his tongue, invading my mouth, his tongue dancing with mine.

Oh my God, I felt I'd been transported into Fifty Shades of Grey with my own Christian Grey. When the fog cleared, I pushed him away.

"What the hell are you doing?"

"I thought that was pretty obvious or have you never been kissed before?"

"You can't do that. I never said you could."

"It's funny, but I don't remember asking," he said, smiling. "And you kissed me back, so I think you liked it."

"No, I didn't," I said, stepping back.

"Well, your lips said otherwise, and you're not going out on a date with anyone. If you need feeding, I'll feed you." He turned towards the kitchen, calling the animals for a toilet break.

We would just see about that. I retrieved my laptop and set up in the corner of the settee, surfing the 'net for shops in the local area. I had a plan.

Jacob came back in, sat at the opposite side of the settee with his phone that looked more like a little computer, I assumed to do business. I kept looking over towards him, but he totally ignored me.

I closed my computer down, refilled my glass, then turned on the TV, all in silence. Around ten thirty, I yawned, put my glass in the sink, then went to bed, without a bye or leave. For Operation Road-trip to happen, I needed to watch and listen.

FIFTEEN

The next morning, I was up a seven, I'd showered and dried my hair, then went in search of some breakfast. I could hear Jacob in the kitchen and could smell coffee. As far as I knew, he hadn't had a shower yet and I was pretty sure he didn't leave the house without one. I entered the kitchen, reaching past him for the kettle, filled it with water and switched it on, all without saying a word.

"How long are you going to behave like a child?" he asked, looking at me.

"I've no idea what you're talking about."

"The silent treatment?"

I just shrugged my shoulders.

"I need a shower, then I've a meeting, I'll drop you at the house before I leave, so you and James can spend some time together. Alexander and Antonio will be about if you need anything."

I just nodded. That was so not going to happen. Jacob frowned, put his cup in the sink, then made his way upstairs. I heard the bathroom door shut but not lock. I waited until I heard the shower running, slipped my trainers on, then slipped my hand into Jacobs jacket to retrieve his car keys. Oh my, the silly man.

I picked them out, popped my head around the living room door frame whispering. "Road-trip guys, who's coming?" Missy and Zeuss jumped off the chair and followed me out of the back door, which I locked and then pocketed the keys. We made our way around to the front of the cottage. Using the key fob, I opened the doors, scooting both animals in, then climbed in myself altering the seat.

"Oh my, guys, how do I start this thing? Wait, wait don't panic. I think I press this button." Ha, so not just a pretty face. The engine purred into life, I looked at the gear stick.

"Well, guys, this should be interesting, it's automatic and I've never driven one, but hey ho, you live and learn. Hold on, guys, here we go." I put it into drive and we were off, just like that. Jacob will definitely not be happy. This will ruffle his well-groomed feathers." I laughed out loud and turned the music up. About twenty minutes later the contraption on the dashboard made a noise and the music went off. I pressed the answer button.

"Molly, get back here right now!"

"Jacob, did you enjoy your shower? It's fab, isn't it?"

"Molly! I'm serious. Turn the car around and come back here now."

"Sorry, Jacob, no can do. Me and the guys are going shopping."

"Molly, I need the car. I've a meeting in an hour."

"Well, Mr. Head of Security should of thought about that when you refused my hire car, shouldn't you. Oh, and by the way, I so want one of these. Never drove such a posh car before, and I must mention I've never driven an automatic before; however, I like living on the edge. You're fully comp, aren't you?"

"Molly!" he shouted.

"Oh my, Jacob, are you losing your cool? So unprofessional." I giggled and pressed cancel on the gadget.

"Oh dear, guys, I don't think our Jacob is a happy guy, but never mind, we have a whole day of fun ahead." Not five minutes later the gadget rang again, the user display said Alexander.

"Yes, brother, dear? What can I do for you? I must say I do like this high technology. I need to get one of these."

"Molly, get back here right now!" That bit I understood; however, it was followed by a string of Italian that left me a bit lost.

"You lost me after the word 'now'. Alexander, I don't speak Italian."

"Jacob's not happy. When he gets hold of you, I can't vouch for your safety. Now be a good girl and come back, you've made your point. It's not safe to be out on your own."

"But, I'm not on my own. Me and the guys are on a road-trip. I need a new dress for tonight."

"Why do you need a new dress? The one you had on the other night was very nice."

"Because, brother dear, Kade has already seen that one. I need something else for my hot date."

"Get back here now. You're not going out with Kade or anyone else for that matter until we sort this mess out."

"No, and oh yes I'm. Goodbye, Alexander." I disconnected.

"Who the hell do they think they are? They have known me for two minutes and think they have control over what I do and when I do it. Well they can get stuffed, couple of nobs. What do you say, guys? Let's go with John Bishop, everyone is a nobhead."

God, my mouth was turning into a sewer. I needed to rein it in a tad. I turned the music up and pressed the off button on the gadget; no one was going to spoil our day.

I reached town not long after and followed the car park signs. I decided on a multistory and found a space behind a dumpster, so the car was hidden from view.

"Right, guys, this is what we're going to do. Zeussy, you're on the lead. Missy you follow until we can find a pet shop, then we'll buy you a top-of-the-range sexy lead in pink. We'll have something to eat, then we'll hit the shops. How does that sound?" Zeuss barked softly and Missy purred.

Three hours later, loaded up with designer bags (designer bags always make me feel good), with both my friends strutting their stuff with new accessories, we made our way back to the car.

I kept looking behind to make sure I was alone, which I was, and made my way to the dumpster that hid Jacob's car. I clicked the fob as I approached and heard it unlock the doors. I opened the rear door so the guys could jump in. Once they were comfortable, I shut the door. I then opened the driver's side, leaning over to place my goodies on the passenger seat, then turned around to climb in. As I did, I was face to face with Jacob.

"Shit, Jacob. I nearly had a heart attack, don't creep up like that."

"Get in," he scowled. "And move over now before I do the ungentlemanly thing and throttle you. You're an absolute pain in the arse."

"Jacob, language," I frowned. "How'd you find me?"

"Tracker on my car; all expensive cars have them," he said through gritted teeth.

"Oh, right. I'll remember that in the future."

"You do that."

"How'd you get here? What about your business meeting?"

"I drove. Ed took the other car back and I cancelled."

"Oh," I mumbled. "It's safe to say your pissed at me then?" He just looked at me with raised eyebrows and said nothing.

"Well this is fun, don't you think, guys?" I asked looking behind at my two sleeping friends. Jacob looked in his rear-view mirror and frowned.

"I hope you're going to get all the hairs out of my car?"

"Well, I wasn't thinking of doing that. You're the one who cancelled my hire car. If you'd kept your nose out of my business, I wouldn't have borrowed yours."

"You are my business, Molly, from now on in, so get used to it. I've men putting an alarm in the cottage. If you refuse to live on the grounds, I'll make sure you're safe wherever you are. Well, unless I move in with you on a permanent basis," he said with a slight smile tugging at his lips.

"No way! Absolutely, no way. Who the hell do you think you are? You people think you can take over my life? Well, it is just not going to happen."

The next minute Jacob slammed on the breaks and pulled to the side of the road, turning off the engine. Unbuckling his seat belt, he leaned over and grabbed me by the shoulders, pulling me towards him.

"Listen to me, you obstinate woman. Do you realise you could have died yesterday when you slammed your car against that tree? I know this situation is hard to wrap your head around, finding out you have a family that you didn't know about. However, when Francesca died it opened a can of worms. Whatever you may think about Antonio, he does love you. Both he and your birth mother have followed your life every step of the way. They did what they did to keep you safe."

"But they didn't send Alexander away or his brother. I don't even know his name, only that he's James's father. That's another thing. Why is James here and not with his mother and father?"

I could feel the tears coming and tried my best to keep them from falling. Jacob's eyes dropped to my lips as they began to tremble.

"Shit, Molly, don't cry, please." He moved his hands up to cup my face, gently kissing my lips. He then leaned back, looking into my eyes again. When I didn't move or say anything he leaned in again. Now his kiss became more urgent and passionate, his tongue invading my mouth. Without knowing what I was doing, I began to respond. My lips began to hungerly kiss him back and my tongue moved to touch his. He moved my head to an angle so he could probe deeper.

As suddenly as the kiss started, he broke away and leaned his forehead against mine. "Come on, let's get you home and find out where they're up to with that alarm?"

He started the car and we continued in silence, both lost in thought about what had just happened.

~~~~

They'd all but finished installing the alarm when we arrived home. Jacob, forever the gentleman, helped me out the car, gathering my packages and handing them to me.

"You go in while I get Missy and Zeuss." I just nodded.

I needed space and silence to gather my thoughts about my feelings for Jacob and where it could possibly go. Should I cancel going out with Kade or just go with the flow?

An hour later, a gentle knock on the bedroom door woke me from my doze. "Molly, you decent? Can I come in?"

"Yes."

Jacob came in, standing in front of me. "You okay?"

"I think so. Has everyone gone?"

"They just left. I need to show you how to operate the alarm. Then I'll have to go; however, I'll be back later."

"I'm going out, remember? There's no need for you to come back."

"You're still going out with Kade?"

"It's dinner with a friend, Jacob, nothing more. Just because we kissed doesn't mean we're dating." He moved towards me making me lean back on the bed, blocking me there with his hands on either side of my face.

"You're as attracted to me as I am to you. Would you like me to prove it?"

He leaned over me, trapping me under him as his lips found mine. I don't quite know how my arms found their way around his neck or when I first noticed his enormous erection pressing against me, but it did the trick of bringing me out of the mind-blowing fantasy I'd sunk into.

"Stop, Jacob. We can't do this. You need to go."

"Why?" he asked, rolling on to his side.

"Why? Because I don't know you, plus I need to get ready and you've somewhere to go," I said, jumping up.

He stood up, straightening his tie. "We haven't finished this by a long way, and don't get any ideas about Kade. Do you know where he's taking you for dinner?"

"No, he didn't say."

"If you get into trouble ring me and I'll come and get you. I've put my mobile in your phone. It's downstairs on the table."

He looked at his watch, which, by the way, looked extremely expensive. "I'm out with Alexander and Antonio for a business meeting, which should take a couple of hours, but after that I'm contactable. Come, I'll show you the alarm. It's a contact system, therefore you can set it when you're in or out of the house. Always set it, Molly. Please do this for me?" I followed him downstairs, he showed me the alarm, kissed me quickly, and left. I watched him turn around and speed off, he was obviously late.

At six forty-five, I was ready and waiting. I felt good. I'd blown dry my hair with a diffuser, so it was full of soft curls. My dress was a deep red and had a fitted sleeveless body with a full circle skirt, which hit just below my knee and fit me perfectly. My shoes also matched my dress.

I was checking my lipstick when Kade knocked at the front door.

"Wow. You look absolutely beautiful, Molly."

He stepped in, pushing me back against the wall, trapping me there with his hands on the wall either side of my head. Next thing, he bent his head and I felt his lips on mine, nibbling my bottom lip until I opened my mouth, letting his tongue in. Time stood still as my lips again responded to a handsome man kissing me. Oh my God, this couldn't be happening. Stop the planet, I want to get off.

"We could forego the meal and get down to desert, if you like?" he said raising his head and smiling.

I coughed, blushing with my head down.

Laughing he lifted my chin. "Come on, sweetheart, let's go. I'm just messing with you."

We travelled in a comfortable silence, listening to a CD.

"Where are we going, Kade?"

"The golf club. It's about a thirty-minute drive. You okay?"

"I'm good, thank you. I don't talk much when I'm travelling."

"Good." He put his hand on my knee and gave it a squeeze and smiled.

We pulled onto the car park, which was less than half-full; however, it was early evening. But I did see a vehicle I knew quite well. Ed was leaning on the bonnet smiling at me. As we stopped, he sauntered over, opening my door and helping me out.

"Ed, what are you doing here?"

"Hi, Miss Molly. I'm waiting for the bosses, Alexander and Antonio. They're having a business meeting. I was just stretching my legs." He nodded at Kade.

"Ed, thank you for getting the door for Molly."

"That's okay, no problem. Does Jacob know you're eating here?"

"No. Can't say that he does," Kade answered.

"Well, this should be interesting," Ed answered with a grin, returning to the car.

"What did he mean by that?" I asked with a frown.

"Don't know, but I'm sure we're about to find out. Come on let's go in, you're getting cold. You should've brought a jacket." He pulled me close to his side, tucking me under his arm to share some of his warmth.

We entered the restaurant, Kade keeping me close as he spoke to the waitress about our table. I didn't really take much notice as I was too busy scanning the room for my father.

I spotted their table just as Jacob's eyes met mine. If looks could kill, I'd have been dead and buried, alive, and Kade's body would never be found. Oh my, he was not happy. He leaned over to Antonio and whispered in his ear. Antonio looked in my direction, then stood as we approached to get to our table.

"Molly, my dear, you look beautiful." He leaned into me, kissing both cheeks. "Kade, how are you?" He reached out his hand to shake Kade's. Alexander also rose and did the same.

"Very sexy, Molly. Jacob's not happy with you, sis," he whispered in my ear. Jacob didn't stand, he just glared. The other four gentlemen stood, waiting for an introduction. However, I had the feeling they already had a good idea who I was, because I felt the hairs on the back of my neck prickle.

Antonio turned to the man who was clearly the leader. "This is my next-door neighbor, Molly. Just moved in, comes from the north of England. My grandson has become very attached to her."

Starting with the leader, I shook each of their hands very firmly. Antonio deliberately didn't give their names and I didn't ask.

Kade also shook each of their hands, then put his arm around my waist. "You ready, sweetheart?" He turned to Antonio. "Enjoy your dinner, sir." With that, he gently guided me to our table.

As we sat, the waiter handed me a menu and I looked at Kade. "Well, that was a bit awkward."

"Mm. What's with you and Jacob?"

"I don't understand. What do you mean?" I said looking at the menu.

"He's attracted to you. I've never seen him behave with a woman like he does with you. I like him and I don't want to step on his toes. I'm also attracted to you, but it's your decision, Molly. I want more than a friendship, as you've already guessed. However, enough about that now, let's enjoy our meal. What would you like to eat?"

I reached over and rested my hand on his. "Thank you."

We smiled at each other and continued to peruse the menu. "Can I just have steak and salad with a side order of homemade chips? I'm not a big eater so a starter would spoil me for the main, but you can have one. I don't mind," I said, shutting the menu. "Who are the people that Antonio is meeting with?"

"Don't know, but they look dangerous. I think I'll have the same. What do you fancy to drink?"

"G and T please. Is that why you sat over there, so you can watch what they're up to?" I smirked.

"No, Molly, I always sit facing the door. It's in my training."

"Interesting, are you SAS?"

"Why would you say that?"

"I read books about Navy Seals. They always sit facing the door."

"Molly, you have one curious mind set."

"Not sure whether that was a compliment, but I'll take it," I laughed.

The waiter came, took our order, then returned with our drinks. Our conversation being light and fun, Kade flirted and I giggled, enjoying his company. However, I was mindful that all his attention was not focused on me. Because of where he'd sat me, I couldn't see Jacob's table, so I had no idea what was going on.

Our food arrived and we tucked in, the conversation which Kade seemed to control, was my life story. He tactfully steered away from himself. After I'd ate my fill of the steak, salad and a few chips, Kade asked whether I'd like a sweet, coffee, or another drink. I asked for a refill before we settled for the bill.

"I need to go the ladies," I said picking up my purse.

"Okay, sweetheart. I'll settle up and get you another drink." He stood, coming around and pulling back my chair.

"You're such a gentleman. Thank you, kind sir." I giggled and moved around the table following the signs for the ladies.

After washing my hands, reapplying lipstick and buffing up my hair, I turned towards the door only to come up against a giant of a man.

"I think you've taken the wrong turning, sir. This is the ladies."

He just grunted, spinning me around, then lifting me off my feet while putting his big hand over my mouth.

Panic gripped me. I started kicking, grabbing his hair and pulling it. He pushed the door open and made his way to the emergency exit, which was the next door along.

In my panic my shoes kicked off and I dropped my purse. I bit his hand and he cried out but still maintained his grip.

"Stop fighting or I'll hit you, woman," he growled.

I struggled, tried to scratch his face and kick him anywhere my foot could land. He set me on the floor and slapped my face, hard.

Oooh! This wasn't good, was my last thought before I saw stars, then blackness.

SIXTEEN

Jacob looked at his watch. It had been ten minutes since Molly had left for the ladies and something wasn't right. He rose from his seat, excused himself, and went over to Kade.

"What's taking her so long?"

"No idea, I'm just going to check on her," he said, standing.

They both made their way through the swinging doors towards the toilets. They both saw the red shoes and purse at the same time.

"Shit! Shit! Shit!" Kade said, running his fingers through his hair. "Someone's snatched her."

"You should've gone with her. You're a top fuckin' agent. How could you let this happen? She's as good as dead."

"Get a grip, Jacob. I can't fuckin' follow a woman into the loo in a public place. We're at a golf club for God's sake. Who the hell would want Molly bad enough to run her off the road, then snatch her on a night out? What's she worth to these people?"

Jacob was silent, struggling with how much to tell Kade. But at this point he needed his help to get Molly back alive.

"She's Antonio's daughter."

"You're kidding me, right?" he asked through gritted teeth. "Tell me you're winding me up."

"No."

"Does she know?"

"As of yesterday, yes."

"And?"

"To say she was upset, confused, and angry is a bit of an understatement."

"Fuck! Well I'll leave it up to you to tell Daddy that he's just signed his daughter's death warrant. In the meantime, I'm going to call in some favors under the radar, see if I can get a lead. I'll go and speak to Ed to see if he noticed any vehicle that just left the car park." With that Kade stormed off.

Jacob turned and headed back to the table. Antonio and Alexander were now both on their feet. The four other men were still seated.

One of the seated men got a message on his mobile. He looked at it, then handed it to the leader of the group. After glancing at an image on the screen, he calmly handed the phone to Jacob.

On the screen was a picture of Molly. She was in the boot of a car. She appeared to be unconscious, the side of her face was red, and she had a badly split lip.

"What the fuck have you done to her, Kincaid?" Jacob asked, fury in his voice. "If she dies, I'll rip your innards out with my bare hands."

"Now, Jacob, calm down," Kincaid said. "We just needed a bit of leverage for our business deal. How was I to know your girlfriend was a bit of a spitfire?"

"You're dead, Kincaid. I want her back and I want her back tonight," Jacob said between gritted teeth.

"Antonio," Kincaid calmly said, "you know what we want and until you deliver, we'll keep Molly as our guest. Don't worry, she'll be safe. For now. However, the longer it takes to finalize the details on our deal, the longer Jacob here will be sleeping alone. And, to tell you the truth, my son has already taken quite a shine to her. Now wouldn't that be interesting, our two families joined by marriage and grandchildren?"

Jacob saw red. Snatching Kincaid by the shirt collar with one hand, he pulled his fist back to smash it into Kincaid's face. As he did, he heard the click of a gun behind him and felt something jab hard into his side as a warning. Reluctantly, he slowly lowered his fist.

Kincaid shoved him backwards. "Antonio," he growled, "keep your dog on a leash and keep your phone on for further instructions. I'll be in touch." With that the four men left.

Jacob turned to Antonio and Alexander. "I'm going with Kade to see what he can find out. I'll meet you back at the estate when I've sorted out Molly's pets and made sure everything is okay at the cottage." He didn't wait for an answer, he just turned and walked away.

Antonio slammed his hand on the table, then turned to Alexander. "How the hell did they find out about Molly? How did they know she'd be here tonight, when we didn't even know, and how the fuck are we going to get her back? We have a leak, son. Find the bastard and sort this mess out."

Alexander just nodded.

~~~~

Jacob found Kade talking to Ed in the car park. As Jacob approached, Kade turned to him. "It was the same SUV that ran Molly off the road. You with me on this?"

"Yes, let's go. Ed, take the boss and Alexander back to the estate. Keep me informed of what's happening."

"Right, boss."

The two men made their way to Kade's SUV and took off. After around twenty minutes of silence, Kade turned to Jacob.

"Are you okay?"

"No, I'm not okay. We might share a mother, Kade, but we're not sharing Molly. I love her and you need to back off."

"Yes, I've seen the way she looks at you. But I like her, too. If you, Alexander, or Antonio hurt her, I'll do everything in my power to take you down and I'll make you pay. But at the end of the day, it's Molly's decision to make."

"Let's get her back in one piece first."

SEVENTEEN

It had been two days since Molly had been taken. Jacob had moved Missy and Zeuss to the estate, to James' delight, the excuse being that Molly had been called away on business.

Kade couldn't get an angle on where Kincaid was keeping her, and no one had been in touch. Jacob was close to losing it; he couldn't sleep or eat. All he could think about was what they were doing to her, and if he got her back, what state she was going to be in. He entered Antonio's office.

"Anything?"

"No," Alexander answered.

"What the hell are they playing at?"

"They're making us sweat," Antonio said, just as his mobile rang. "Unknown number," he said, as he moved to answer it. "Yes?"

"We meet today," Kincaid's smooth voice said. "Midday, somewhere neutral. There's a derelict farm on Lower Briar Hill Lane, two miles east of town. You know the conditions: Molly in exchange for your agreement to withdraw all business dealings with Kingston Industries." With that he disconnected.

"Jacob, scope out this farm. I don't want any surprises. I want my daughter back alive. We have a lot of catching up to do." With that, he stood up and left the room. Alexander and Jacob followed.

EIGHTEEN

As I slowly became conscious, I became aware of a soft pillow under my head. I could hear male voices speaking quietly nearby.

"Ah, Molly, my dear, finally you return to us. I am so sorry that one of my men got a bit over zealous; however, you're a bit of a fighter."

"Who are you and what do you want?" My voice was a bit raspy as my mouth was painfully dry.

"My name is Kincaid," he answered with a smile. "I am a business associate of your father's. I want him to do something for me and you are my bargaining chip."

"How come everyone knew he was my father except me?"

"That, my dear, is a question you will have to ask him. For the moment you will be my guest. This is my son Ryan. He is going to be staying with you to keep you out of trouble because I feel you could be of considerable trouble if left alone. If your father does not deliver, well, we might have to find a different tactic, like joining our two families together; marriage, children, you know the script. Legitimately, of course."

"What do you mean?" I asked, looking between the two men.

Ryan answered, moving around the bed and sitting down close enough to cradle the side of my face in his big hand.

"You're very pretty, Molly. I think our children would be beautiful, don't you think?"

I turned my face away; however, Ryan brought his other hand up, cupping the other side of my face, forcing me to look at him. He leaned in, kissing me.

When I didn't respond, he forced my lips open and invaded my mouth with his tongue.

"Don't worry," he said as he pulled back. "Once I make you mine, I'll not stray. I'm a one-woman man and you'll be well looked after. I almost wish your father refuses our terms. I want you so badly it hurts."

"You're mad. All of you are mad. Take me home now. I have animals that rely on me. I have a business to run." Unwelcome tears came as I felt panic clutching at my chest. I struggled against Ryan without any effect. He was a big man, just like Kade, Jacob, and Alexander. He had a scar on his left cheek, he was ruggedly handsome. With his long, dark hair tied back, he looked to be ex-forces.

"Molly, calm down, you're having a panic attack and I don't want to hurt you. If you continue to fight, I'll have to give you something to make you sleep again."

Ryan now held both my hands in a tight grip, stopping my struggling. He started kissing my neck, whispering soothing things in my ear. After a few moments, my struggling slowed, and my breathing had returned to normal. When he felt me relaxing, he turned my face to him and invaded my mouth again.

On the other side of the room, Kincaid laughed as he pressed his mobile to his ear. "Antonio, did you receive my picture? That was just to prove how serious I am. Mid-day and no surprises."

He left the room leaving us alone. Ryan stood, releasing me. "Go and wash up in the bathroom. there are some sweat pants and a t-shirt for you to change into. We'll be moving in an hour." He moved to the window with his back to me.

"How long have I been here?"

"Two days," he answered, not turning.

"Two days? I've been out for two days?"

"With a little help, yes. You must need the bathroom and something to drink. Go do as I ask, or I'll have to assist you."

I turned, locking myself in the bathroom, but doubted that the flimsy lock would keep Ryan out if he really wanted to get to me. As I washed up and slipped into the oversized clothes that had been left for me, I took in the bathroom, looking for an escape route, but found none – no window and no other door.

Shit, I was in trouble. When I thought about starting a new adventure, this was not what I was expecting. If Alice knew what was going on, she'd have heart failure. I looked in the mirror, putting a finger to my split lip and running my fingers through my hair.

When I returned to the main room, I could smell fresh coffee and toast.

"Where are we?"

"It doesn't matter," he said. "We're leaving soon. Eat something or you'll get sick."

"What does it matter to you if I get sick. I'm going home."

"You think?" he asked, turning to look at me. "I want you for myself. I've been watching you for years at my father's request. His mistake. I'll not let anything happen to you because you'll be my wife and bear my children. Mark my words, Molly."

"But I don't know you, and I most certainly don't love you, so how can that work? You do know this is the twenty-first century and not the nineteen forties?"

He laughed. "Come on, eat up. We have to go meet your father."

"I'm not hungry and I've no shoes."

"Eat, I said, and you don't need shoes, I'll carry you."

I managed a few bits of toast and a few sips of coffee, before there was a knock at the door.

Ryan pulled a gun out of his waistband and looked through the security eye-hole in the door before opening it.

"Molly, let's go and please behave. My father's men are not as gentlemanly as I am, as you well know."

Ryan picked me up and carried me down corridors and stairs, depositing me in the back of a black SUV. I was beginning to think everyone on the planet owned one except me.

We travelled in silence along the country roads for what seemed like miles. Finally turning off down a dirt track, we travelled for another mile or so, coming to a stop at an old farm building. There were several cars parked in front, one of them I recognized. Ed was leaning against the bonnet.

Ryan climbed out, coming around to open my door. He lifted me out, then carried me into the building. Putting my arms around his neck, I pulled myself up to look over his shoulder, raising my hand in a little wave to my friend Ed.

As we entered what looked like the kitchen, Antonio and Kincaid were seated opposite each other at a table, flanked by Alexander, Jacob, and two of Kincaid's men. Jacob didn't look happy, especially as my arms were wrapped around Ryan's neck, which I suppose gave the impression of intimacy, adding in the fact I was without shoes and was wearing a man's t-shirt and sweats.

Kincaid got to his feet. "Ah, Molly. Ryan, put her down. We have come to an agreement."

Ryan didn't respond, he just looked at his father. "Ryan," Kincaid said more firmly, "put Molly down."

He slowly lowered me to my feet, whispering in my ear. "I'll come back for you, Molly." With that he turned and left. There was the sound of a slamming door and a car speeding away.

Jacob immediately came towards me, lifting me into his arms. He nodded to Alexander, then turned, taking me out to the waiting car. Ed was now behind the wheel.

Five minutes later, Alexander climbed in the passenger side and Antonio came into the back with Jacob and me. Jacob had his arms tightly wrapped around me. No one spoke and the journey home was made in complete silence.

"Molly, wake up, you're home." Jacob whispered.

"I'm not asleep," I said, my anger starting to boil over. "And this isn't my home. I'd like to go to my home and the next time I see any of you will be a minute too soon!"

Antonio spoke up. "You're my daughter and you'll do as you're told. Jacob take her upstairs. I'll arrange for the doctor to make a house call. After you've been checked and had a rest, we'll have dinner and discuss your future."

I bounced up off Jacob. "Now, you listen to me," I said, "and listen well. You are not my father! A father has to earn that right. I don't know you from Adam. The father who raised me is dead, along with my mother. I want to go home to the only family I have left and that's my pets."

"Don't speak to your elders in that manner and your family, as you call them, are here. Jacob take her upstairs and lock her there if you have to."

"Don't you dare, Jacob!" I warned him.

Alexander opened the door and grabbed me around the waist, lifting me out. Jacob followed, taking me from Alexander, and throwing me over his shoulder.

I started kicking, screaming, and thumping his back with both my fists. "Let me down, you jerk."

He ignored me and kept on up the steps and through the door to the stairs.

"Molly, stop it now or I'll take you over my knee."

"You wouldn't dare."

"Just watch me, sweetheart. Now behave."

He went through a door which opened into a beautiful bedroom with an enormous bed, with matching everything – pillows galore, old style old oak furniture and the type of carpet that you just sank into, like floating on air.

"Wow!"

"Good, you're lost for words," he said putting me down. "The bathroom's that way; however, I think you should see the doctor before you take a bath and change."

"Why?"

"You know why."

"No, I don't know."

"He needs to examine you."

"What for?"

"To see if you've been, um, well, you know what I mean."

"No, I've no idea what you're talking about."

"Fuck, Molly, do I've to spell it out for you."

"Yes, Jacob, because I've no idea what you're talking about."

"Violated."

"Raped, you mean?"

"Yes."

"Don't you think I'd know if I had been?"

"We have no idea what they've done to you. You've been missing for two fucking days; two days in which I've been sick with worry about what they were doing to you."

"Well they didn't rape me, okay? They knocked me out in the beginning, but Ryan was nothing but courteous. He didn't let anyone hurt me."

"Ryan? Ryan held you prisoner for two days against your will, he's his father's son. So, don't get any ideas about good old Ryan, he has an end game."

"Just like Antonio and Alexander, and Kade, and you, then?"

"I'm not arguing with you. You're home safe, you'll wait and see the doctor, then I'll run a bath for you."

"You're not staying and I'm not seeing the doctor. I want my animals back, then I want to go home."

"Jesus, you are one stubborn woman."

Just then there was a knock at the door. "Molly, Doctor Sinclair. May I come in?"

I arched an eyebrow. Jacob turned, striding to the door to let the good doctor in.

"Molly," he said, "I hear you've been in the wars again?"

"Yes, doctor," I answered, "but not of my making."

The doctor turned to Jacob. "Can you give us a minute?" Jacob nodded and left.

"Sit, Molly, let's have a look at you."

The one thing I could say about the good doctor, he was thorough. After about twenty minutes, he decided I was sound.

"Did they touch you intimately?" he asked.

"No."

"Can I examine you?"

"No."

"How can you be so sure when you were unconscious for two days." he said gently.

"Believe me doctor, I'd know."

"Okay, Molly, I can't force you. However, if you change your mind, come to my surgery."

"I will, doctor."

"One more thing. Are you aware that I brought you into the world?"

I looked at him in surprise. "You're older than you look then."

"I was twenty-five and new to the area, when I was called to my first home birth. You were a beautiful baby and have turned into a stunning and well-grounded woman. Please look after yourself. If you need me for anything, just call me."

He rose then, moving to the door. As he left, I heard him talking to Jacob in the hall, before the door opened wider and Jacob came in.

He went to the bathroom, ignoring me. I heard the water running so he was obviously running me a bath.

I followed him into the bathroom. "I can do that myself, I'm not an invalid. I need to be on my own. Will you please leave?"

"No, I'm not leaving you on your own." He came to stand in front of me. "Why would you not let Dr. Sinclair examine you fully?"

"He had no right to discuss that with you."

"He didn't. I asked if you'd been raped, his answer being, you'd said not, which indicated he hadn't examined you."

"Sneaky, Jacob. Very sneaky." Feeling tired and defeated, I asked,

"Can I be on my own please? I'm not going anywhere. This place is like Fort Knox."

He stared at me for what seemed like ages, I held his eye contact – I was sure he was trying to read my thoughts, whether he could trust me to do as I was told. He suddenly nodded, stepped around me and left. I smiled. Big mistake, Jacob, big mistake.

I turned off the taps, returning to the bedroom, making my way to the wardrobes. I needed shoes. After a frenzied search I came up empty handed. "Shit!" I muttered, sitting on the floor venting my frustration. Well, nothing lost, nothing gained, as they say.

I stood up, moving to the double doors, which I presumed led to a balcony. They were locked, of course, however the key winked at me, sitting in the lock. I smiled as I turned it and the lock clicked. I slipped through the doors, closing it behind me.

I stood and thought for a moment. Mm, I should lock it and take the key. I turned, retrieving the key and locking the door.

Moving on to the terrace I looked over the railing. Not a big drop, but I could do some damage if I fell awkwardly. There was however, drain pipes running down both sides to the ground.

I pulled on them testing how secure they were. Deeming them solid enough, I decided I'd go for it. Rubbing my sweaty hands on my pants, I climbed onto the balcony ledge, grabbed the pipe with both hands, pulling myself off, and started to shimmy down.

~~~~

After leaving Molly to take her bath, Jacob made his way to the security office, where one of his men monitored the cameras twenty-four seven.

"Brett," Jacob said to the security officer, "angle the rear camera onto the back terrace where I've left Molly."

Brett nodded. "What are you looking for, boss?"

"Just watch. She thinks I can't read her like a book."

They watched as the petite figure of Molly came out of the bedroom doors, shutting them. She then turned, going back in, but returned almost immediately, locking the doors with the key. She then checked the drain pipe before climbing up, swinging her legs across, then clumsily climbing down.

"What are you going to do, boss?" Brett said, turning just as the door closed behind Jacob.

~~~~

Halfway down, I seemed to be stuck. I looked down as I tried to move, but my foot couldn't find another bracket. "Ooooohhh," I moaned out. "I don't think this was a good idea."

Just then a voice I recognized answered from below. "No, it wasn't. What the fuck are you doing? Let go and I'll catch you," he shouted up angrily.

Just then Alexander appeared, followed by Antonio and James, with Missy and Zeuss in tow.

I turned to face the wall, hanging on for dear life. The strength I was using to climb down was slowly slipping away. I knew I was going to fall unceremoniously to the ground. I look down again focusing on James.

"Molly, what are you doing up there? Is it a game? Can I play? Are you coming or going?"

The innocence of a child, I thought, as giggles bubbled in my chest. As I started to laugh, my hands slipped, sending me down to the ground. Fortunately, two strong arms caught me before I hit the flagstones on the path below.

James ran to me. "Molly? Molly, are you okay? Are you playing hide and seek with Jacob?" I looked at Jacob's angry expression, then down at James.

"Yes, James, that's just what I was doing, but don't you try it until you're at least twenty-eight." I ruffled his hair.

Alexander looked over with a smirk on his face, shaking his head. "Come on, James, let's go inside and let the grownups talk." With that he shuffled the boy and animals back towards the house.

Jacob looked down at me, still in his arms. "Grownup is a bit of a stretch as far as you're concerned. Where the hell did you think you were going, woman?"

"Home."

Antonio stepped forward. "This is your home."

"No, it's not. Please, I just want to go back to the cottage, with my pets."

Antonio was silent for a minute, then turned to Jacob. "Take her to the cottage and stay with her. We'll discuss the future tomorrow. The animals can stay here for tonight."

Antonio turned to the house, mumbling in Italian. Jacob walked around the house to the SUV parked at the front, putting me in the passenger seat and strapping me in. Slamming my door shut, he climbed in the other side. He then started the engine and drove to the gates, which opened as we approached.

"How old are you again?" he turned to me and muttered. "Because you're acting like a spoiled teenager."

"No, I'm not. I've managed for twenty-eight years without you and my mob family interfering in my life, so I'd rather you all just butt out, thank you very much."

"Well, unfortunately for you that's not going to happen. It's known who you are and now you're on everyone's radar. You, sweetheart, have a target on your back."

"This is so fucked up. I should never have come here. Whatever was Francesca thinking leaving me the cottage?"

Jacob turned to me. "Perhaps, sweetheart, she just wanted to bring you home."

The car pulled to a stop on my drive. I unclicked the seat belt and reached for the door handle, only to have it swing open. "Kade, what are you doing here?"

"Came to make sure you're okay, Molly." He nodded at Jacob who opened his door to come around to my side, however Kade had already lifted me out. I wrapped my hands around his neck and rested my head on his shoulder.

"Mm, you smell nice."

"Thank you," he smiled at me and then at Jacob.

"I'll take her, you open the door," he said holding the key out to Kade.

"I've a better idea, bro, you open the door, and I'll take her in." Jacob was about to say something but thought better of it.

My house was lovely and warm. I breathed a sigh of relief as Kade lowered me to the sofa. God, it was good to be home.

I felt a bit jaded and dirty. I just wanted everyone to leave so I could run a bath and soak with a nice glass of wine or something stronger.

Kade knelt in front of me gathering my hands in his. "Molly, are you okay? Do you want me to get you something, run you a bath, something to eat?"

"No, I'm fine, I'd just like to be on my own please, if you don't mind".

Just then Jacob appeared. "That's not going to happen; I'm staying. I'll run you a bath. Kade, I'll take it from here."

Kade stood and turned to Jacob. They glared at each other, but eventually Kade backed down, saying he had somewhere to be, but he'd call in tomorrow to check on me.

After he left, I heard Jacob lock the front door, put the new chain on and set the alarm. I then heard him go upstairs and then the taps were running.

I went into the kitchen and poured myself a glass of wine, before returning to the living room and putting the surround sound onto my favorite music. I sat on the couch, leaned my head back, and closed my eyes.

~~~~

Several minutes later, Jacob was shaking me awake. "Come on, Molly, your bath is ready. He leaned over and lifted me up in his arms. I snagged my wine glass as he lifted me and carried me upstairs.

The bathroom was full of steam, the bath was full of bubbles with tealights all around, and the main light was off. He lowered me to the floor and turned me towards him.

"Molly," he said as he lowered his lips to mine. They were close, but not touching. "I like you and I know you're attracted to me. I want to see where this can go. Are you willing to give me a chance?"

I closed the space between us, wrapping my arms around his neck, running my hands up through his hair. That was all it took before his lips were on mine. What started off soft and intermittent, soon turned to hot and invasive. His hands cupped my face, turning my head so that his tongue could invade my mouth. His hands ran through my hair, then moved down, caressing my neck, then moving down my arms. With his one hand on my neck and one on my behind, his mouth never left mine. After several minutes of this, we came up for air.

"Well?" he asked.

"Yes, please."

His hands moved to the bottom of my t-shirt. My eyes never left his as he lifted the shirt over my head and threw it on the floor. He reached behind me, unhooking my bra, as he leaned down, taking my lips again. He then reached down, slipping my sweat pants and panties down. He knelt down, removing them, but instead of getting up, he leaned in, kissing my stomach and running his hands up the cheeks of my behind.

I threw my head back and moaned, "Oh my God."

I was so turned on. I thought I was going to have an orgasm there and then. Running his hands down my legs, he brought his hand around and ran his fingers between my thighs, briefly touching my core.

He then stood up, unbuttoning his shirt, stripping it off, followed by his trousers and boxers. Both standing naked, he then lifted me up and placed me in the bath. As I sat down, he climbed in behind me. I relaxed against his broad muscular chest, while his arms wrapped around me making me feel safe. I closed my eyes and sighed.

"Jacob, what's happening? Three months ago, I had a normal boring life. In the last week I've been run off the road, kidnapped, discovered my mum and dad are really my aunt and uncle. From living hand to mouth, I now own a beautiful cottage and have money in the bank, enough that I don't have to work again. I'm scared. I can't live at the estate; I need my freedom. I'm a free spirit. I've been looking after myself for years."

"Listen to me, sweetheart, relax, we'll work this out, and I'll be with you. I'll protect you with my life. We'll work this out together."

I looked up at him over my shoulder, the next thing his lips were on mine, invading my mouth. Not breaking contact, I turned around, sliding my hands behind his neck, reaching up to run my fingers through his hair. Water seeped over the top of the bath, making puddles on the floor.

He groaned with deep desire. Pulling his head back, he whispered. "Molly, you're killing me sweetheart. I want to make love to you so badly."

"What's stopping you?" I moaned.

With that, he stood, lifting me up in his arms, stepping out of the bath. He lowered me to the floor, grabbing a fluffy towel off the radiator, he started patting my skin dry whilst nibbling at my ear and kissing my neck. He then lifted me up and carried me into the bedroom.

Lowering me to the edge of the bed, he knelt in front of me, cupping his hands around my face, leaning in to kiss me. He started off softly with butterfly kisses, but they soon turned hot and passionate, as though he couldn't get enough. His mouth moved to my neck, making his way down to my now very erect nipples.

Taking one in his mouth he sucked and bit gently. "Oh my God," I moaned. He moved across to my other breast and gave it the same attention. Moving down, he kissed my stomach, sliding his hand down to where his lips had been on my tummy, to hold me down. His lips leaving a burning trail until his tongue licked the soft folds between my legs, he eased my legs wider to gain more access. His tongue then invaded me. Gently at first, but then with greater urgency. Never in my life have I experienced anything like it. My hands reached down to run through his hair.

"Jacob." He stopped, looking up at me.

"You do know I've never, you know, been with a man before?"

"Molly, relax, I know. By the time I take you, you'll be ready. I want the first time to be special. I won't lie, it will hurt a little in the beginning but that will pass, I promise."

As he was talking, I felt him gently inserting a finger inside me. The feeling on intense pleasure was so mind blowing I couldn't think straight.

"Oh God, Jacob, that feels so good." He ran his tongue through my folds again and inserted a second finger. I felt the orgasm start from my toes, making its way up my body until I saw stars. I'd read about them, but oh my God, I never thought I'd experience this kind of mind-blowing sensation.

"That's it, Molly, come for me baby. You're so wet, you're nearly ready."

He kept his hand on my tummy as I tumbled over the edge, screaming his name. He then stood. My eyes moved from his face to his very, very, large penis. I looked from that to his face with scared eyes, then back down again.

"Mm, Jacob."

"Yes, Molly."

"Are you sure that's going to fit?"

He chuckled and said. "It will fit, don't move and let me do all the work."

His lips crashed into mine. His tongue invaded my mouth, as he entered me. I gasped, and he stopped.

"Molly, just breathe and the pain will pass. Tell me when you're comfortable. He waited for a minute until I nodded, then slowly, oh so slowly, he eased inch by inch further into me. I could feel his length filling me, stretching me, and my body tightening around him.

"Oh God, Molly," he moaned. "I can't last much longer. Are you okay?" I threw my head back and nodded.

With that he started to move, slowly at first, but as I started to moan, approaching another orgasm, his rhythm increased until the passion took us both over the edge. I felt him exploding inside me, and his lips found mine.

After several minutes, he rolled over, pulling me with him. He was still inside me, his erection giving no sign of receding.

"Molly, that was amazing."

"Mm."

Jacob just laughed. "I can't believe you're lost for words?"

"Really?" I smirked, then turned serious.

"Jacob, Ryan Kincaid said he was coming for me."

Jacob stiffened, wrapping his arms tight around me. He lifted my chin and said, "Let him try."

"Who is Kincaid and what did he want with me?" I asked.

"Kincaid was business partner's with your father some years back. When a deal went bad, Kincaid left Antonio to take the fall. It cost him a lot of money."

"Ryan said he'd been watching me for years. Why would he do that?"

Jacob was silent for a while. "I can only assume that Kincaid has been aware of your existence all this time and has waited until he could use you as a bargaining chip when needed."

"So, what happens now?"

"Well, if Ryan has a thing for you, we'll have to find him and sort this mess out. Which will mean you'll have to move on to the estate for now."

"I won't do that, Jacob. I'm sorry, but that's not going to happen."

"You're just being childish now. Do you want this to happen again?"

"So, what are you saying? Life as I know it is over? I must be a prisoner and give up my freedom, all because my father is a gangster? A father, I might add, that I've only known for approximately a month?"

I jumped out of bed, grabbing my discarded clothes, pulling them on in a temper. I turned my back on Jacob and stamped out of the bedroom.

I made a cup of tea, opened the back door and sat outside, pondering what I was going to do next. I was so lost in thought, I jumped when I heard Jacob's voice.

"Molly, you can't run away from this. You can do everything you do here up at the house, only with added security. When we have the situation with Ryan under control, you can move back here and carry on as normal."

"That's until some other slime ball climbs out of the woodwork. I won't live like that. Coming here was a big mistake."

"Well, you're here now. You can't turn the clock back, so you'll have to suck it up and get on with it."

"Thank you, Jacob, for those pearls of wisdom. The first thing I need is a set of wheels, so I'm going to ring the insurance company and tell them I need a courtesy car."

"No, I've told you, going out alone isn't safe. You'll have someone with you, either me, Alexander, or one of my men."

"I'm not arguing with you over this, so get over it," I said standing and pushing past him.

I set about making something to eat. Jacob closed the door, staying outside on his mobile. After around twenty minutes, he came inside, coming behind me and putting his hands around my waist. He leaned in, kissing my neck.

"Molly, I'm only trying to keep you safe, I care about you and don't want you getting hurt."

"I know, Jacob, but you can't keep me under lock and key. I need my freedom. I don't want to get involved in any shady business. And that's another thing, you and Kade are very cozy, what's the story there?"

"There's no story, we're friends."

"Really?"

"Yes, really."

"Well, Antonio and Alexander think he's dangerous, and investigating both them and you."

"I know."

"So, being friends doesn't complicate matters?"

"No, why should it? Kade knows what I do for a living, and as long as I don't break any laws, we don't have any issues."

"Fair enough," I answered.

"Molly, I have to go out for a while. I've some business I need to deal with. As I go, I want you to lock the doors and put the alarm on. Don't let anyone in."

"I'll be fine, Jacob. Stop worrying."

He turned me to face him, well his chest actually, as he was several inches taller than me. He bent, capturing my lips, moving his hands to tangle in my hair.

"I'll be back in a couple of hours. Please stay out of trouble."

"I don't know what trouble I can get up to in here. Go. The sooner you go, the sooner you'll get back," I said, following him to the front door.

"Lock the door, Molly, and put the alarm on, like I told you to."

"Right. Go, for God's sake." I shut the door, put the chain on and went to the window, watching him reverse out of the drive.

I grabbed the insurance documents off the sideboard, looking for a contact number. Finding it, and my policy number, I rang them.

After a couple of minutes of music in my ear, a young man came on the phone. "How can I help you?"

"My boyfriend rang a couple of days ago to report an accident I had. I'm ringing to see if my policy covers me for a hire car for the short term?"

"Yes, it did, Madam; however, that no longer applies as the claim has been settled. According to these notes, a colleague spoke to your fiancé. Due to its age, your car was deemed too expensive to repair.

A sum was agreed upon and a check has been put in the post to you."

"Oh, well, thank you. Sorry for bothering you. Jacob is away on business, so he will probably ring me later with the details. Thank you again."

"Shit," I muttered to the empty room. "What am I going to do now?" I loved my car. What a bloody mess. Well, tomorrow I'd commandeer a car. I was sure my father and Alexander had more than one that I could borrow.

My mobile rang again. "Hi, Alice."

"And where have you been hiding? I've been trying to get hold of you for a week."

"How long have you got?"

"Well, I'm home alone, with a glass of wine, so as long as you want. How are the two hotties?"

"Well, long story short. Alexander's my brother. Antonio's my biological father. Kade's a secret agent, well, not as in James Bond, and Jacob has asked me out. I've been run off the road and my car's a write off. I've been kidnapped by thugs, but I'm home safe now. I think that just about covers everything. How's your week been?"

Silence.

"Wow! You're joking, right? Go back to the beginning and start over, nice and slow."

"It turns out that Francesca, my grandma who left me the house, and Antonio, who is Alexander's father, were an item. I was conceived, but given to Francesca's sister when I was born, to raise as her own, as Antonio is a bit shady, and they wanted to keep me safe. Therefore, Alexander is my half-brother, along with Antonio's other son who lives in Italy, who I might add is James's father, but I've yet to be given his name."

"Right. And you know this, how?" Alice piped up.

"Well, when I was run off the road by some thugs, it was deemed I had a need to know."

"Okay, so, moving on. Kade's a secret agent?"

"When I asked Alexander why he had flirted, knowing he was my brother, he said he did it because Kade was showing an interest in me, and that he'd been keeping an eye on the whole family for years."

"Okay, so Jacob and you are a couple? How did that happen?"

"Well, we've been flirting for the last couple of weeks. I don't know, I just felt a connection with him. He's sexy, a hunk, protective. I just feel safe when I'm with him."

"Wow! You blow me away. You don't do anything by halves, do you? Have you had sex with him?"

"Alice!"

"Well?"

"I might of," I giggled.

"Well, sister, congratulations on losing your virginity. At twenty-eight no less." We both laughed. "So, what happens now?"

"No idea. I'll just go with the flow, I guess. But no way am I going to move into Antonio's house. So, it's anyone's guess how Jacob's going to react to that. We'll see."

"Well, girlfriend, it's all happening. My phone is low on battery, so I'm going to have to go. Molly, be safe. Listen to your gut and stay out of trouble. I don't know why I'm wasting my breath, but we love you and we don't want to see you get hurt, physically or emotionally."

"I know, I know. I love you, too. We'll speak soon. Bye."

I sat back and closed my eyes, pondering the last couple of weeks and what I was going to do. Jacob hadn't returned. Were we really a couple, or was it a fling? I was new to all this, I needed clarification. I was tired and frightened, plus I was missing Zeuss and Missy. The cottage felt big, lonely, and too quiet. I reached for my phone again and dialed Jacob.

"Molly, what's wrong?"

"Nothing, I'm tired so I want to go to bed. You said you'd be coming back but the door chain is on. You won't be able to get in."

"Don't worry about that, leave the chain on, and turn in. I won't be long now."

"Okay, well if you say so. Night."

"Night, Molly."

After putting my phone on charge, I checked the doors and alarm again. I then went upstairs, had a quick shower, and climbed into bed.

NINETEEN

The next day came all too soon. I could smell fresh coffee, so I assumed Jacob was back. As to how he had gotten past the chain was anyone's guess. When I walked into the kitchen, he was sitting at the dining room table, surrounded by paperwork.

"Morning," I said with a sleepy yawn. "What are you doing?"

He grabbed my hand and pulling me onto his knee. He then gave me a slow kiss that curled my toes.

"Working."

"They look like accounts. I thought you were head of security?"

"I am. I'm investigating something."

"Do you want me to have a look? After all, I do accounts for a living."

"No, I don't want you involved."

"Are you breaking the law?"

"No, Molly, I'm not breaking any laws," he said with a laugh. "Why do you assume I'm always breaking the law?"

"Well, you all look a bit shifty to me." Still sitting on his knee, I grabbed his face in both hands. "Jacob, I need to ask, only because I'm new to this. Are we a couple, you know, after yesterday?"

"You mean because we made love? I don't go around jumping into bed with every woman I meet. To answer your question, yes, I'd now class me as your boyfriend."

"What will Antonio say? Will it affect your job?"

"No. Both Antonio and Alexander know how I feel about you, plus the fact is, I've already spoken to your father."

"You did what? Now just a minute. I don't answer to Antonio or anyone else. As far as I'm concerned, I run my own life. My parents died years ago and even they wouldn't have a say in who I did and didn't sleep with."

I pushed off his knee and walked over to the cupboard to retrieve a cup, pouring myself a coffee. "So, what are you up to today?" I asked, changing the subject.

"Well, I have some business to sort out. I'd like you to go up to the house and spend time with James."

"I've things to do as well. I have to bake a new batch of cakes for Albert, and I've some accounts to do. So, I can't do that."

"You can do that at the house."

"No, I live here, everything I need is here. All I need is Zeuss and Missy back. You're not keeping them hostage, are you?"

He just laughed and shook his head.

I pondered whether to mention my car, but I thought that would alert him to the fact I wanted to go out. He'd then arrange for someone to take me and babysit, and that just wasn't happening. He started gathering the papers and putting them in his briefcase.

"Right, I'm going now. I've arranged for Eddie to come and get you, but if you're staying here, I'll tell him to stay until I get back."

He walked over trapping me against the unit, bending down and kissing me. He eventually let me come up for air, which was good because I was running out of oxygen, fast. God, he was a good kisser.

"Right, okay, go on, go. You're going to be late."

He looked at me with a frown.

"What?" I asked, raising my eyebrows.

"Nothing, that just seemed a bit too easy. Normally it's harder to get you to comply."

I opted not to respond, afraid I'd give away my intentions.

"I'll ask Eddie to bring your pets back." He leaned down to give me a final kiss, then left.

I checked the store cupboard and found I was low on just about everything, which meant I had to get to a shop before I could fill my next order for Albert. However, with no car, I was a bit stuck. I could go on my bike, it had a basket, but I'd be limited on what I could buy. I suppose I'd have to wait for Eddie, he'd know where the nearest supermarket was.

TWENTY

It was a good twenty minutes later when I heard a car pull in to the drive. This was quickly followed by a firm knock on the front door. I opened it to find Eddie's smiling face.

The next minute, I was knocked to the floor by an overzealous Zuess, who proceeded to lick my face. Missy then sauntered past, obviously ecstatic at being home.

"Nice to see you too, Missy," I laughingly shouted after her. Eddie then helped me to my feet and shut the door.

"Are you okay, Miss Molly?"

"I'm fine, Eddie. Would you mind taking me to a supermarket so I can grab some supplies?"

"No problem, but I'll have to check in first with Jacob or Alexander. They said if you wanted to go out, I had to let one of them know where we were heading."

"Okay, you check in. I'll go and find my handbag and shoes." I filled the animals' bowls with food and water, retrieved my shoes and coat, snatched up my bag, and met Eddie back at the front door.

"Did you speak to Jacob?"

"No, it was his voicemail. Alexander isn't answering either. I've left a message for Jacob. So, let's go."

Eddie helped me into his car, which was another black SUV. I wasn't quite sure whether I had to get in the back, but Eddie opened the passenger side next to him.

As Eddie drove, I settled back, listening to the music on the radio and watching the beautiful countryside pass me by. Eddie and I chatted comfortably. I found out he had a girlfriend, who he was mad about, and he was hoping to propose to her at Christmas. I also found out he'd worked for my father, or Antonio should I say, for around ten years.

"Eddie, tell me about my mother."

"Francesca was a beautiful person inside and out. Everyone loved her, she was just like you, very arty. In fact, you look just like her. Your hair coloring, your height, eyes, everything. You could be her twin. When Antonio looks at you, well, I can't imagine what he's thinking. He was heartbroken when she died. You can have all the money in the world, but you can't buy your health."

"Are there photographs of her somewhere?" I asked.

"I imagine there'll be some at the house. Have you looked in the loft?"

"No, not yet. That's on my to do list. I didn't see any photographs at the estate when I was there. Why would Antonio hide them?"

"I've no idea. Perhaps you should sit down with him and ask all the other questions you have. As your father, he's the only one who can help find the answers you seek."

"How long have you known he was my father?"

"The minute I set eyes on you."

"So, that being said, everyone locally that has met me will have guessed?"

"Pretty much, yes."

The rest of the journey passed in a comfortable silence. I was lost in thought and didn't notice when Eddie pulled into the car park of a large supermarket chain. He pulled into a space, jumped out, and came around to open the passenger door to help me climb out. With my little legs it was rather like a free fall to the ground. Eddie caught me and chuckled.

"Easy now, Miss Molly."

I grabbed a trolley, and sauntered through the doors, thinking that Eddie would wait at the car for my return. No such luck, I turned around to a big Eddie smile.

"Sorry, Miss Molly I can't let you out of my sight, Jacobs instructions."

I just shook my head and smiled. Eddie had no idea what he'd committed to. It wasn't unusual for me to wander around a supermarket for hours. I don't do lists because I don't buy the same items every week, I buy whatever takes my eye. So, an hour and a half later, as I approached the check out with a frustrated Eddie trailing behind me, I smiled up at him and winked.

"God, Molly, how many people are you buying for? Are you expecting visitors?"

"Well, you're babysitting me during the day, Jacob has the night shift, and Alexander and Kade keep appearing out of nowhere. I must be prepared to feed everyone. Plus, I have some baking to do for Albert at the shop." He helped me start unloading the trolley, then went to start packing at the other end of the checkout.

One hundred and thirty-nine pounds later we made our way to his SUV. If it was going to cost me that much every week to feed everyone, I was going to start charging them. I was so deep in thought that I didn't realise Eddie had stopped until I ploughed into the back of him.

"Oh my God, Eddie, I'm so sorry, I was miles away. Is there something wrong?"

"No, let's just get this shopping loaded and get back to the cottage."

I don't know what had spooked Eddie, but something had. I looked around, but nothing seemed off, so I just followed him to the SUV.

Instead of letting me help pack the shopping, he opened the passenger side door, lifted me in, and closed the door. He then left me to get comfortable while he loaded the shopping into the back.

Five minutes later we were on the return journey, but Eddie kept checking his mirrors, which was making me really, really, nervous.

"What's wrong?"

"Nothing, Molly, relax. It won't take long to get home."

"You're making me nervous," I said, turning towards him. "You keep checking your mirror, plus something spooked you in the car park."

"I thought I saw someone I knew, but I might've been mistaken. Relax we're fine and we'll be home soon."

I lapsed into silence, looking out of the window at the scenery.

As we approached the cottage, I noticed Jacob's car was on the drive. When we pulled up, Jacob opened my door and lifted me out, setting me on my feet, and planting a soft kiss on my lips.

"I got Eddie's message. You've been shopping? Couldn't you have waited until I got back? You know, it's not safe to go swanning about until I find out what Ryan Kincaid's up to."

"Jacob, I'm not putting my life on hold. I've commitments to people and I've run out of baking supplies and other essentials. Plus, you've left me without transport."

"Which was done on purpose, for exactly this reason. If I hadn't, you would have gone off on your own and we probably wouldn't have seen you again." He gently guided me to the front door.

"Open up, Eddie, and I will bring the shopping in," Jacob commanded. I frowned at him, while he just raised his eyebrow in response.

After hanging up my coat and putting the kettle on, I started putting away my shopping. I heard the front door close. I turned as Jacob entered the kitchen.

"Has Eddie gone?"

"Yes, I sent him back to the estate. Antonio wants to speak to you." He came towards me putting his hands on my shoulders, pulling me in for a hug.

"I know what he wants and it's not happening."

"Molly, just listen to what he has to say; he only wants to keep you safe."

"The only reason I'm not safe is because of him. It's a bit late now."

Holding my face in his hands, he silenced me with a toe-curling kiss.

"Mm, should we move this upstairs?" he whispered between kisses.

Laughing, I stepped back. "I'd like to say yes, however Albert is calling in a couple of hours, so I have to start baking. Which reminds me, where did you sleep last night and how did you get past the door chain?"

"I slept for a couple of hours next to you. I was on top of the quilt, so as not to disturb you. I don't need a lot of sleep. As for the chain, well, that's on a need to know, and you sweetheart, don't need to know."

I smiled up at him. "Right then, I better get started. What are you going to do?"

"I've some calls to make. After Albert leaves, we're going up to the estate for dinner."

Before I could reply, he lifted my chin, kissed me and walked off into the living room. "No argument, we're going, Molly."

I gave a huge sigh, turned, and started collecting my ingredients to make choux pastry for my eclairs.

Albert arrived around four thirty, handing me an envelope of money. "That's your share of the takings, Molly, I've never done so much business. You're one hell of a baker and an asset to my little shop. Rumor has it that you're also a bookkeeper. I don't suppose you could help me out with mine before year-end?"

"No problem, Albert, would you like Jacob to help you getting this latest batch in your van?"

He looked over at Jacob. "Would you mind?"

"No problem," he said as he stood.

TWENTY-ONE

An hour later, I was showered and changed. Jacob helped me into his SUV.

"Jacob, what's James' father's name?"

"Micelle, and he's your brother, a fact you need to embrace, sweetheart."

The gates opened as we pulled into the drive. I turned and waved at Eddie who was back in the gatehouse.

"When will I meet him?" I asked, as we stopped in front of the house.

"Soon. You're taking a trip to Italy in the next couple of days." With that he jumped out of the car, coming around to help me out.

"What! Why? Who with?" I spluttered, stepping back from him. "I can't. I don't have a passport and I've Zuess and Missy to look after."

"I'll sort out your passport. Zuess and Missy will come here while we're away."

"No! No! I can't go. I don't want to go."

"Why? Think of it as an all-expenses-paid holiday with your family."

"I'm not going, and you can't make me."

128

"We'll see. Come, both your father and your dinner are waiting." With that, he guided me forward, his hand on my lower back.

As we entered the dining room, Antonio was pacing up and down while speaking on his mobile. He stopped speaking immediately and disconnected.

"Molly, you look beautiful, just like your mother." He hugged me, giving me a kiss on each cheek.

"I don't mean to be rude; however, seeing as there is no evidence of her even existing, I'll have to take your word for it."

Antonio moved towards a display cabinet at the far side of the room. Picking up a photo frame he returned and handed it to me.

I took it and looked down at the picture. It only took a split second for the world around me to disappear. I felt my chest tighten as though I couldn't breathe. Black spots appeared before my eyes, then just blackness.

~~~~

I don't know how long it was before I could hear voices of concern around me.

"Molly, are you okay?"

I opened my eyes to find Jacob leaning over me.

"What happened?"

"You fainted."

"Well, that's a first and I'm still not flying."

"Why?"

"I don't like flying."

"I thought you said you had never been on a plane?"

"Well, I might've lied just a tad."

Jacob raised his eyes at me, turning to Antonio and Alexander who had now appeared.

"I think she'll be fine." He bent down and wrapped his arms around me. "Come on, I'll help you up."

As I was helped to my place at the table, I looked around for the photograph that had mysteriously disappeared again. Looking over at Antonio, I asked, "May I keep the photograph of my mother?"

"It obviously upset you, are you sure?"

"Yes."

He nodded. "If you are sure, yes, you may. I'll give it to you after you've eaten."

Maria brought in our meals and there was silence as everyone tucked in. I played with my food until the silence was deafening.

"Why are you going to Italy?"

"*We* are going to Italy. I always take James home before he starts his new term. I also have some business meetings. You, my dear, can't be left behind as Jacob and Alexander are coming as well. We don't fly commercial; we have a private plane, so, we'll be able to work on your fear of flying."

"What do you mean you have a private plane? It costs a pretty penny to have your own plane."

He laughed. "Don't you worry about it, dear, it's tax deductible."

"I can't go anyway," I said smugly. "I don't have an up-to-date passport."

"You'll have one tomorrow, so you'll need to pack."

"What? No! I don't want to go. I've things to do here. You can't just run rough-shod over my life, whether you're my father or not. I haven't set eyes on you for twenty-eight years. What gives you the right?"

"What's so important it can't wait until you return in a week?"

"Well, lots of things. I need to go shopping for a new car. I bake for the local shop and I have my pets to look after."

"Nothing that can't wait then. We agree, yes? Jacob will sort out your passport and see that you have suitable clothing for the visit to your brother."

"Now hold on one minute," I said, placing my knife and fork down on the table. "I've never in my adult life been told what to pack for a trip. I'm certainly not starting now."

Alexander decided to step in, I assumed because he spotted steam coming out my ears. "Molly, relax. Eat your dinner and drink some wine. All Antonio meant, although he didn't explain it very well, is we have some important engagements to attend for which you would be expected to wear dressy evening wear. If you don't have any in your wardrobe, we need to purchase some."

"You *are* going, Molly, as I'm not leaving you here alone with Kincaid on the loose," Jacob's no-nonsense voice piped up beside me. "Now eat and enjoy."

Turning to Antonio I leaned my chin on my hands, elbows on the table. I realized how rude it was, but hay hoo.

"So, tell me about Kincaid and why his son has such an interest in me."

Antonio just looked into my eyes as if trying to make a decision. He took so long I thought he was going to ignore me.

"When I was a lot younger, Kincaid senior was my partner. We worked together for years doing this and that, that's not really important. Kincaid became a wee too greedy, betrayed our agreement, and left me to take the fall. He knew about your mother and me. When you were born, he must have kept tabs on you, knowing that at some point he could use you to his advantage. You mentioned that Ryan said he'd been watching you for years and that he'd become attracted to you. Well, the only thing I can think is that as you became older and more self-sufficient, his father felt that Ryan was the only one he could trust to keep an eye on you. It's the only thing that makes any sense."

"Okay, so what happens now?"

"Well, Jacob is trying to find out what Kingston Industries have that Kincaid is so eager to get his hands on. Then we neutralize Ryan Kincaid."

"When you say neutralize, what exactly do you mean?"

"That, my dear is none of your concern."

"I don't like the sound of that."

"Molly, just leave all this to me. You don't have to concern yourself. It's only business, something I'm good at."

"If you're talking about killing people, it is my business. Father or not, I want no part of it. Ryan was very kind to me. I'll not stand by and let you take matters into your own hands." With that I stood. "Thank you for dinner, but I want to go home now."

"Sit down, my dear, you've hardly touched your food and you are far too thin."

I pushed my chair in, searched for my purse, and made for the door. As I reached for the handle, I felt two hands grab my shoulders. Jacob leaned in to my ear. "Molly, come and sit down; you need to eat."

"No, Jacob, I can walk home. It's only next door for God's sake. You stay, I'm sure you have things to discuss. You know, like crimes to plan, drugs to peddle, weapons to sell."

"Where the fuck did all that come from?" he said, stepping back.

"I don't know, where do you think, Jacob? My so-called father just said he's going to neutralize someone. Take a step back and listen to yourselves." With that I left.

I stormed down the hall, and out of the front door, making my way to the gate. Eddie was standing at the end of the driveway waiting for me.

"I have to take you home, Molly, and stay until Jacob gets back."

"I don't mind you walking me home, Eddie. However, once I'm locked inside, I'm sure I can look after myself. I've been doing just that for eighteen years."

He only laughed and shook his head. I always felt comfortable with Eddie so, as we walked the short distance to the cottage, I started to quiz him about Antonio's business.

"So, I believe Antonio has his own private plane. I take it he's not short of money. What kind of business is he in?"

"Haulage and transport across the globe," he said and smiled.

"As in drugs and weapons?"

"Now, Molly, I never said that."

"I know what you said, but you have to be honest. You were a bit vague."

Just then we stopped at the front door. "Molly, key?"

"I can do it. Before you go, Eddie, they've told me that I must go to Italy with them. What do you think?"

"I think you'll be safe with Jacob. And why not, a free holiday for a week, on a private jet. Go for it."

"Thanks for bringing me home, Eddie. I'll be fine."

I stepped through the door, closing it, before Eddie had a chance to step in. I locked it and put the safety chain on. I then slid a cabinet that was in the hallway across the door, blocking anyone's entry. If Jacob could get through the safety chain, I'm sure someone else could. Well, that wasn't happening.

I called the guys for a toilet break, then locked the back door, and put a dining room chair under the handle. After everyone was settled, I mounted the stairs and changed into my PJ's and climbed into bed with a book.

I always sleep with the windows open. Having never lived in the country, I couldn't get used to the total lack of traffic noise.

It was so relaxing, it was hard to believe there was evil in the world. The UK was so beautiful when the sun was shining. Everywhere was green, luscious, and the birds were singing.

~~~~

I woke early to a beautiful summer's day. I opened the curtains and peered out. "Oh my, that's not good, guys."

Jacob's SUV was in the drive. The man himself was leaning against the bonnet on his phone. Well, I thought, he's just going to have to wait until I'm showered and dressed, and I'm not rushing.

Moving the cabinet back to its normal spot, I unhooked the chain and opened the door, leaving it ajar for Jacob to enter. I made my way to the kitchen, removing the chair and unlocking it, letting Zuess and Missy out. I felt Jacob behind me as I filled the kettle.

"Why did you do that?"

"Do what?"

"Come on, Molly, stop behaving like a child. Shall we start with your tantrum up at the house, storming out, then locking me out."

"I didn't lock you out, you don't live here. I made the house safe for me and the guys because you're giving me paranoia about being kidnapped by God knows who. This isn't my world, Jacob. I don't like it."

"Well, sweetheart, you're going to have to get used to it because there's no going back. Plus, have you forgotten that we're a couple?"

"Just because we had sex once and shared a couple of kisses doesn't mean you can move in and play happy families."

Jacob didn't answer, he just pulled me into him, kissing me as though his world was going to end in the next couple of minutes. I must admit he did have my toes curling. He eventually let me up for air.

"Tell me you didn't enjoy that, Molly, and want more?"

"I've nothing to compare it to."

"And you won't. Now let's go and pack your things. We've had to move the flight forward to this afternoon and you need to get the animals settled at the house."

~~~~

As I was going through my wardrobe, I suddenly realised that I hadn't seen Kade in a couple of days.

"Have you seen Kade? I haven't even heard his bike go past in the last few days."

"No, I haven't heard from him. You good to go?"

"Just have to get Zuess and Missy sorted. What about my passport?"

"All arranged, babe. Come on stop worrying." He leaned in for one more passionate kiss, then grabbed my case.

"I thought I needed to go shopping?"

"No time. We can sort that when we get to Italy."

"But won't clothes be expensive there?"

"Don't worry about the cost."

I grabbed the guys' bowls, leads, and food, then followed him out. I waited while he made sure the alarm was armed and the door was locked securely.

Jacob stowed everything in the boot, then came around and helped me climb into the passenger side; these SUV's weren't meant for little people. After the animals were comfortable, we made the short journey to the house.

As we entered, it was a hive of activity. James was so excited. Zuess latched onto this and started jumping up at him, until Jacob commanded him to stop. Funny, he never did that for me when I shouted at him, it must be the testosterone of the male species. Missy just sauntered past to the kitchen; obviously us girls know were the best treats can be found.

I followed, hoping to find Maria to apologize for having the added inconvenience of looking after my pets. As usual she waved off my apologies, saying she was paid well, and she loved their company.

Leaving Zuess and Missy begging for treats, I shut the kitchen door and went outside to find everybody. Two SUV's were now parked at the front and James had already strapped himself into the one that Jacob used.

Smiling, he leaned out the door, shouting to me. "Come on, Molly, we're in this one with Eddie and Jacob."

I looked around for Jacob, but he was talking to Alexander and Antonio.

Eddie was closing the boot, then he turned and gestured for me to climb in the back. After helping me in and gently closing the door, he climbed in the passenger seat. I had to admit to myself, all the men here had impeccable manners.

I leaned forward, poking my head between the front seats. "I thought you were staying here, Eddie?"

"Change of plan, Molly. Jacob thought we needed extra security, seeing you were all taking the trip."

I raised my eyebrows at James, settling back, making sure we were both strapped in.

Jacob climbed in behind the wheel and we were off. It was around an hour's drive before I saw the airport sign. We turned off on to a side road.

"What airport is this?" I asked no one in particular.

"Private air field," came the response from the front.

Oh, I didn't like the sound of that. I didn't like flying at the best of times, but private airport meant a small plane. Likely one with propellers that needed to be started by a handle at the front, or that's what I was imagining in my tiny brain. I so wanted to go home to my nice cozy house and snuggle up with my pets. I could feel myself starting to hyperventilate; this was definitely not good.

"Stop the planet, I want to get off," I whispered to myself.

We pulled up beside a hanger. Jacob and Eddie jumped out; James followed. I remained in my seat, looking out the window.

In front of me was a small executive passenger jet. Okay, it didn't have propellers but, in my mind, it still didn't look safe. No way was I going all the way to Italy in that little plane.

Jacob opened my door. "Molly, come on, get out."

"Err, don't think so, I want to go home. I've changed my mind, I'm not going."

"Yes, you are. Come on, climb out." He undid my seat belt and lifted me out, planting me on my feet. He put his arms around my neck, leaning in for a kiss. I shut my eyes and hugged him close. A blackness descended, then nothing.

TWNETY-TWO

The next thing I could hear were voices, however they weren't near enough for me to make sense of them. I could, however, feel someone breathing close to my face. I opened one eye to take a peek.

"James? What are you doing?"

"I'm waiting for you to wake up, Molly. Antonio said I wasn't to disturb you, to let you wake up on your own."

"Where are we?"

"We're on a plane, going to Italy, don't you remember?"

"Vaguely. Where is everyone?"

"Working on business."

"James, can you speak Italian?"

"Of course, Molly. I was born there."

"Do you think you can teach me? I mean secretly. I'd like to surprise Jacob. It would be like a game."

"Ciao, Molly, il mio nome è James."

"Ciao, James, il mio nome è Molly."

"Cool, Molly! We're on our way," James giggled.

I grinned. Yes, James, I thought, now I just have to remember it.

"James, I need to speak to Jacob."

"He's back there, should I take you?"

"No, sweetie, you wait here and watch the film. I won't be long."

I removed my safety belt, stood, and made my way to the back of the plane. Knocking on the door, I opened it and popped my head around.

"Molly, you're awake, come in. I'd like you to meet some of the key members of my network." Antonio stood up to greet me, kissing both my cheeks.

Besides Jacob, Alexander, Eddie, and another two members of Jacob's men that I knew by sight, there were two other men, both dark, tall, and dressed in business suits. They also looked like they worked out and looked after themselves, although not as muscular as Jacob and Alexander.

I nodded at them as they stood, making their way around the table to shake my hand. Both had very firm hand shakes. I think you can tell the type of man you're dealing with by their hand shake. If they thought my grip would be weak, they were mistaken.

"Hello, Molly, nice to meet you, my name is Bernard. I'm your father's accountant. Your father tells me you are also into finance? Does this mean you'll be checking my work?" I don't know whether there was a veiled threat in his question or whether he was just fishing.

"And why would I do that?" I asked with raised eyebrows. I didn't much like this man.

"I was just teasing you." He then stood back. The second man took my hand.

"How do you do? I'm Jon, your father's personal advisor."

"Nice to meet you both. Jacob, could I've a word, please?"

Alexander stood and hugged me. "You okay, sis?"

I nodded and smiled at Eddie. Turning, I left the room, hoping

Jacob was following me. I heard the door close behind me.

"What's wrong, Molly?"

"You drugged me. You know like BA Baracus in the A-Team?"

"Pardon?"

"Never mind."

"I didn't drug you. I used a pressure point on your neck to make you sleep. I knew you were panicking about the plane journey, so I eased that panic."

I looked into his eyes to see if he was lying to me; however, all I saw was honesty. Well, I think that's what I saw.

"I need the ladies' room."

He frowned looking over my shoulder. "It's behind you."

"I know that. The last time I used the toilet on an airplane, I set off the emergency alarm. Can you show me where it is, so I can avoid the embarrassment again?"

Jacob threw his head back laughing.

"It's not that bloody funny. Just show me, I'm bursting."

Still laughing, he shook his head, grabbed my hand and pulled me towards the restroom.

"There, sweetie. You would have to pull the string."

"Right, thank you."

I turned and pushed him out the door, locking it. I've never been so relieved in my life. I washed up and made my way back to James. We settled down to watch Marley and Me. As per usual, I ended up in tears.

After the film finished, I asked the young man who was looking after us to refill my gin and tonic and James' juice. James then switched to the music channel while we updated ourselves with the latest top forty. I began to relax while listening to the music

The thought of landing in this minuscule aircraft was making my heart beat twice its normal rate. There was a ping on the intercom system and all my senses sprang to alertness.

"What's that about, James?"

"I think it means we'll be landing soon."

As he answered, the seat belt sign came on and I could hear movement behind us. Jacob's head appeared over our heads.

"James, change seats, son, so I can sit next to Molly."

He smiled at Jacob. "Okay, I'll go and sit with Grandfather. Molly, if you need me to hold your hand, just shout."

Jacob laughed. "I'm going to hold her hand, James. Don't you worry about Molly."

Jacob made himself comfortable in the seat next to me, then leaned in for a kiss. "Miss me, sweetie?"

"Not that you'd notice." I smiled back. I leaned forward to root in my bag.

"What are you looking for?" He said raising his eyebrows.

"My sunglasses."

"Aren't you a bit premature, we haven't landed yet."

"No! I'm just getting ready. My mum, the one that brought me up, always had her keys ready a mile before we reached home. It's in my upbringing."

Jacob just shook his head and smiled. But then he saw what I'd pulled out of my bag. "What on God's earth are those?"

I looked down at my lap. "My sunglasses."

"They're purple with pink roses on!"

"So?"

"They're big and round."

"And?"

"They'll cover most of your face."

"Again, and?"

"They're very sixties."

"Again, so?"

"Well, have you no Ray-Bans?"

"Jacob, you are such a snob. No, I haven't got any Ray-Bans, besides these are prescription sunglasses. Alice says they're so me."

I smiled up at him. He towered above me even sitting down. I heard the landing gear being lowered so I grabbed Jacob's hand.

"It's okay, Molly, I've got you." He leaned over, cupping his other hand around my cheek, kissing me softly.

"I know I'm being silly, but I can't help it. I hate taking off and landing."

"We'll be there soon. Close your eyes and breathe."

The plane started dropping fast. Within a minute, the wheels hit the tarmac smoothly and the engines roared as they went into reverse. My nails were digging into Jacob's hand. I felt, rather than saw, as I had my eyes closed, him leaning in to give me a kiss that was toe curling. Boy was he a good kisser.

"There, nothing to it, we're here," he whispered. "Now stay seated until I make sure everything is ready for our transfer to the waiting vehicles. Am I clear?"

"Yes, sir." I raised my eyebrows and frowned. Did he think I was a child?

"Good girl."

I very childishly stuck out my tongue out at him as he released his seat belt and stood, smirking at me.

The next fifteen minutes passed in a blur, as everyone packed laptops away. The doors were released, and I assumed stairs were brought for us to disembark. James had now moved back to the seat beside me as we waited for further instructions. Like good girls and boys.

"Oh my God, James, I feel like I'm on a school trip. Do these people know that I'm a grown up?" James giggled beside me.

"I think Jacob knows because he keeps kissing you. I think he loves you."

Now it was my turn to giggle. "Don't be silly, we've only just met."

"I heard him tell grandfather that he had every intention of marrying you at the earliest opportunity."

"You did? When was this?"

"Just before we left the house."

"Well, that's news to me."

"Don't say anything because then they'll know that I'm listening to them when I shouldn't be. Promise, Molly, please?"

I leaned over giving him a hug. "I promise. It's our secret, as long as you promise to teach me to speak Italian secretly." We just grinned at each other. Pact made.

Everyone passed us as they left the airplane. Eventually Jacob came back in.

"Molly, James, come on let's go. Let Eddie go first, James hold Molly's hand. I'll be right behind you."

"God, Jacob, is all this coat and dagger stuff really necessary?"

"Yes. Humor me."

We followed Eddie out under the blue skies of Italy. Then the heat hit me. Oh my, was it hot. I pulled my sunglasses from the top of my handbag and slid them on. Looking down at James, giving his hand a tug, I smiled.

"Wow! Molly, you look like a movie star with those glasses on. Cool."

I threw my head back and laughed. My thoughts going back to Jacob's view on them.

As we reached the tarmac, James let go of my hand, running forward.

"Daddy, Daddy!" He ran to a tall, muscly man with long black hair tied back in a ponytail. He wore figure-hugging jeans and a white shirt open at the neck. His skin was the color of mocha and he had the most beautiful smile as he lifted James in the air, giving him a huge hug. They both started speaking in Italian, so the exchange was totally lost on me. I turned my head taking an interest in what was happening with the other people milling around. I then felt a hand at my back.

"Follow, James, sweetheart."

As I walked forward, the man I assumed was Micelle turned towards me, putting James down, keeping tight hold of his hand.

"Molly, so nice to meet you finally. You're as beautiful as your mother." He pulled me into a bear-hug, kissing both cheeks.

Ping!

The next thing, I found myself face down on the tarmac, Jacob's body covering mine.

"Molly, are you okay?"

"Yes, I think so. What was that?"

"A bullet. You need to get in the car with James and Antonio. Head down. Go, now!"

As I dove into the car and settled in the far corner, I heard Jacob yelling orders to everyone. Micelle climbed behind the wheel, Alexander jumped in the passenger side, then we sped off.

I turned in my seat. "Where's Jacob?"

Antonio leaned over, patting my hand. "Doing his job, Molly. Stop worrying. He'll meet us at home."

I turned to the front and watched the countryside slip by. Well, slip was slightly understated. I couldn't quite see what the speedometer was reading, but I was pretty sure it was in the red area.

Micelle and Alexander were quietly talking in the front. Antonio was shouting at someone on his mobile. James was looking at me, then down at my leg.

"Molly, you're bleeding."

"What? Where?" I asked looking down.

"Your leg."

Peering over my sunglasses. "Oh, so I am. I must've hurt myself when I hit the ground."

"But there's a lot of blood, Molly."

Alexander leaned over the seat. Antonio disconnected his call, unfastened his seat belt, and moved over to examine my leg.

"Bullet wound," he said. "I won't be able to tell if it's still in there or just grazed the skin until we get you home."

I looked up at Alexander. "I think I'm going to be sick. I want Jacob. What if I die before he gets back?"

"You're not going to die, Molly, but we do need to get it seen to, quickly. Were nearly there now."

"Alexander, the others are coming up fast behind us." Micelle nodded towards the rear-view mirror. "You going to tell Jacob about Molly?"

"No. He can't do anything if we do. Just get us home ASAP."

Just then my mobile rang. Looking at the screen, I saw Kade's number.

"Now, stranger, where have you been? I've missed you."

"Molly, where are you? I've been to the cottage and it's all locked up. Zuess and Missy aren't there."

"Italy."

"Italy, and what are you doing there?"

"Just landed. I was told I'd be safer here with the rest of the family. But I'm thinking someone was lying to me."

"And why do you say that?"

"Well, there was a bit of an incident."

"What kind of incident?"

Just then I caught my leg against the door handle, sending excruciating pain up my leg.

"Molly! What's the matter?" I didn't answer as I closed my eyes to fight the nausea. Oh God, I was going to be sick. Alexander was waving at me to give him my phone.

"Molly? Molly!"

"It's alright, Kade, I'm here. I think the bullet hit my leg."

"Put Jacob on right this minute," he shouted angrily.

"Can't do that because he's not here. And you're not helping by shouting."

"Where the hell is he?"

"I think he's driving the car behind us. He stayed behind to find out who was doing the shooting."

"Right, this is what I want you to do. Find something cotton like a handkerchief, fold it to make a pad. Press it down on the wound. Then find a belt and fasten it round it to hold in place."

"Okay but were nearly at Antonio's house now."

"I don't give a shit where you are, do as you're told." With that he disconnected.

"Hello? Hello? Well, he's one happy bunny," I muttered.

Throwing my phone in my bag, I leaned over, snatching Antonio's hanky out of his top pocket and folded it as instructed. I pressed it down on my leg, the pain causing me to hold my breath for a couple of seconds.

"Does anyone happen to be wearing a belt?" I asked.

"I am, Molly. You can borrow mine." James wriggled in his seat as he unbuckled his belt and handed it to me.

"Thank you, sweetie."

I fastened the belt tight around the padding, then settled back in my seat.

The wireless phone connection rang in the car. It was Jacob.

"Alexander, what the fuck happened to Molly and why wasn't I told?"

"Because we've only just spotted that she was hurt, plus there isn't anything you can do. The bleeding is contained and we're nearly at the estate. She'll be fine. She's my sister, you know; were on it."

The connection went dead. Oh my, another unhappy bunny. The world was full of them today.

We turned through a bend, coming to a stop in front of some very large security gates, which were attached to the Great Wall of China. Well, that's the nearest similar thing I could come up with.

"Wow, they're huge! What goes on behind these walls, a scientific experiment?"

I was leaning between the two front seats, my leg forgotten. Both Alexander and Micelle looked at me and frowned.

I shrugged. "Just saying."

The gates opened automatically, so I assumed there were cameras watching our arrival. Micelle started to drive through.

"Stop!"

The car stopped; Alexander turned to me. "What's the matter now?"

"Once you get me in here, will I ever be allowed to leave. Or is it like Jurassic Park?"

James was giggling behind me. Alexander shook his head.

"Micelle, drive, ignore our sister. She has a warped sense of humor."

"Like I said, just saying." I turned to James and winked. Antonio just shook his head smothering a grin. "I think he likes me."

Micelle said something in Italian to Alexander, who replied similarly.

I leaned back, whispering to James. "What did he say?"

He whispered back, "He said Jacob's got his hands full with you."

"Well, that's just rude."

We pulled up in front of the most beautiful villa I've ever seen. However, I didn't have much of a chance to take it in, as my door was yanked open and Jacob leaned in. His face was not happy, he looked like he had swallowed a wasp, or maybe a bee, as the saying goes.

"Molly, you told me you were okay. What the hell are you playing at?"

"Calm down, it's only a scratch. Did you find the shooter?"

"No, we didn't."

"Well, I don't think it was the Kincaids," I stated.

"What makes you think that?"

"It was a last-minute thing, me travelling with you, that is. So I think it's an inside job and I think it's your accountant."

Jacob shook his head. "I think you watch too much television. Come, I'll carry you to our room and see to that leg."

"Well, he doesn't like me, and I think he's cooking the books. Hang on a minute. Who says we're sharing a room?"

"I do. That way I can keep an eye on you. You're like a magnet for trouble."

I just huffed. Turning to Micelle I apologized for bleeding all over his car. Jacob undid my seat belt, lifting me into his arms, leaving James to follow. Micelle shouted to Jacob in Italian.

"What did he say?"

"He said I must be a saint."

"Ignore him, he's just so rude. I think it's in his genes." Jacob just shook his head and laughed.

"Come on, let's have a look at your leg."

I wrapped my arms around Jacob's neck. He lifted me out and we entered through the front entrance. He made his way straight to the stairs, which were made of a rich oak, and climbed them as they arced onto the next level. My head swiveled to take in the beauty of what I was seeing.

"Oh my God, this is so beautiful. If this is just the hall, what will the rest of the house look like?" I turned back to Jacob, just watching him silently. We reached a door at the end of a hallway.

"What?" Jacob looked at me.

"You're very good-looking."

"And you're very beautiful. A handful, but beautiful all the same."

With that he kissed me, never losing stride as he entered the room, or should I say suite. He kicked the door closed with his foot. I came up for air as he placed me on the bed.

"Right, take your trousers off while I get the first aid box from the bathroom."

"What, no foreplay?"

"Molly, be serious. I need to see how bad your leg is. I don't understand how you didn't know you'd been hit."

"Well, I was in shock at the time. Plus, I had my sunglasses on, so the blood didn't register until James mentioned it. It's the first time I've been shot at in my life so forgive me for not taking in all the finer details."

He came back and sat beside me, looking at my leg, his eyes moving up my body until he reached my eyes.

"Were you just looking at my underwear?" I accused.

"It's very nice underwear."

"I know, but you're on nurse duty at the moment, so keep your mind on the job at hand."

"True. Let's have a look." With that he was all business.

"It's a scratch, Molly. I'll clean it and put on a fresh bandage. It will be healed in a couple of days."

After he'd finished, I opened my suitcase, found some fresh chinos, and put them on.

"Right, should we find the others?" I asked.

"If we must. I'd rather just take you to bed. However, somehow I think someone would come searching for us."

I liked this fun side of Jacob. Oh my, I think I was falling for this guy in a big way, despite his autocratic ways.

As my wound was only classed as a scratch, I was allowed to walk under my own steam back down the magnificent hallway and stairs in Jacob's wake. As we walked, I tried to take in all the beautiful furniture and pictures.

Chesterfields and a huge brick fireplace filled the main lounge area. Lovely bronze statues sat on old mahogany dressers. The floors were all marble. Very chic. However, try as I might, I didn't spot a TV anywhere.

"Whose house is this?" I felt like the host on Through the Keyhole. I tried to hide my smile as I followed behind Jacob.

"It's the family's, however Micelle lives here mostly."

"Oh, with James' mum?"

"No. She died in child-birth."

I stopped short, putting my hand over my mouth. "Poor James and Micelle, of course, that goes without saying. How awful. That explains why he spends a lot of time with his grandfather. He's never mentioned either to me. He doesn't seem to be affected, he's very intelligent and well-mannered for a young man his age."

We entered the kitchen area, very modern and homey. However, it was full of very large men. I stayed behind Jacob, lost behind his size.

"Where's Molly?" Micelle asked.

Jacob turned, frowning. "She was here a minute ago."

He grabbed my hand and pulled me in front of him. Which was exactly what I was hoping to avoid. Everyone stopped and stared at me.

"Hello," I stuttered.

Antonio stepped in with the introductions. "Gentlemen, this is

Molly, my daughter. Molly, these gentlemen work for us and will be looking after your safety while we're here. I'd much prefer if you would not wander off unless you have either Jacob or one of us with you."

"So, you're saying I'm on lock down for the duration of my stay?"

"I'm not arguing with you about your safety."

I raised my eyebrows and glared in his direction. I heard a muffled cough from somewhere, however I just glared at Antonio.

Saved by Michael Bublé, my mobile started to sing. I'd pocketed it before we'd come down the stairs. I reached in my pocket pressing the connect button. Not looking at the screen, I answered.

"Hello, Molly speaking."

"That was very formal, is this a bad time?" Alice's voice had a cheeky tone to it.

"No, your timing is perfect."

The next thing, my phone was snatched out of my hand by Jacob, who then looked at the caller ID.

I turned, jumping up at his raised hand, trying to retrieve it. When I missed, he grinned. I saw red and planted an elbow in his middle. Not expecting it, he doubled over, which is when I snatched the phone back. Stomping on his foot, I turned to the open back door, making a quick exit.

"Alice? Are you still there?"

"Yes, what happened? It sounded like you attacked someone."

"Only Jacob. He tried to be a smart arse. He's not laughing now though."

"This couple thing is going well then?"

I laughed. "We'll see."

"So, how are things?"

"Well. Someone shot at me, gave me a bit of a scratch on the leg."

I took a seat at a patio table. I then heard movement at the side of me and Eddie plonked his muscular body next to mine.

"Excuse me one moment," I said into my mobile.

"Eddie, what are you up to?"

He smiled at me. "Watching your back, Miss Molly."

I frowned at him and returned to my friend. "Sorry, carry on, I've an ear wig."

"What? Who?"

"Eddie, my friend and Jacob's second in command."

"Right, that's it. I'm coming down to sort these people out, as you obviously can't. I'll be there on the next train."

"No, you can't. I'm not in England."

"What do you mean? Where the hell are you?"

"Um, Italy."

"Italy? How the hell did you get there? You haven't got a passport."

"Well, apparently I do now. Not that I've seen it or even had to show it to anyone. We came in by private jet, to a private air field."

"Well, obviously not that private as someone tried to kill you."

"Mm, point taken."

"Right. Where are you? I'll get a flight."

"Just a minute." Turning to Eddie. "Where are we?"

He laughed and shook his head. "Tuscany."

"Tuscany?"

"Right, I'm on my way. I'll text you with the flight details."

"Wait! Alice, wait!" I looked at Eddie. "She's gone. Oh my. She says she's on her way. And believe me, she's a force to be reckoned with when she's on the war path. What should I do?"

Eddie just shook his head and grinned. "Well, I'd start with telling your father to expect another guest."

"No, we'll not be staying here. I'll book us into a hotel. We're going to have fun. I don't think fun is a word my family is familiar with," I said, laughing.

"Have you forgotten what happened at the airport?"

"No, I haven't. But I don't think they were shooting at me. No one even knows I'm here. I think it was a case where I was standing in the wrong place at the wrong time."

"Good luck with getting that past Jacob and Alexander." With that, he stood and went inside.

TWNETY-THREE

The kitchen was empty, so I kept wandering until I heard voices and followed the sound. I came to a door to what looked like an office which stood slightly ajar. I knocked and the voices inside stopped.

"Come in, Molly."

"Micelle, Alexander, what're the plans for the rest of the day?"

"Well, we have some business to attend to. James is swimming and Jacob's making some calls. So, it's up to you, although I recommend you don't go swimming for a couple of days until your leg heals."

"Read, draw, paint, or just relax by the pool. We're not going out again today. We normally eat around eight, if that's okay with you?"

"That's fine. I'll do my own thing then." I backed out the door, giving them a little wave.

~~~~

I collected my sketch pad and pencils from the bedroom and made my way back to the pool, peering into a few rooms along the way. Not that I'm nosy or anything.

As I found a table to park myself, I waved at James. Settling down to draw, my mobile pinged a message.

Arriving tomorrow afternoon, Florence Airport, Peretola around 3pm. Be there...

I smiled and texted back.

Looking forward to seeing you. Boy are we going to have some fun. Not staying here though. Look out for me as we might have to run for it and lose my bodyguard.

I sat back and pondered a plan of action. It wasn't going to be easy to get out of those gates. Getting transport to the airport unnoticed would be even harder.

Putting some music on my phone, I relaxed into the chair, sketching without really concentrating. James popped his head over the side of the pool.

"What are you doing, Molly? Who's that playing on your phone?"

"Rag'n'Bone Man. Do you like it?

"Yes, turn it up louder."

"Your wish is my command, young sir," I smiled. "James, you're turning red. Let me put some more sun cream on you."

He climbed out, and I reached to the sun lounger, retrieving the sun cream. A thought suddenly struck me.

"James, you know at home you have a way of getting over to my house without alerting anyone. Is there a way out of here without going through the gates? Like a secret door?"

"There might be, but it's a secret."

I chuckled. "But it will be our secret."

I finished smothering him in sun cream, standing behind him, with my back towards the pool. He stepped back when I wasn't expecting it, forcing me to take a step back. The next thing, my arms were waving to try and reclaim my balance and failing.

As I hit the cold water, I let out a scream. I hit the bottom, turning, then pushing my way to the top. By this time, James had jumped in to save me. I broke the surface, laughing. I grabbed him and threw him into the air. By this time, we were both laughing.

Two suited gentleman I'd never seen before stood at the pool edge; however, after a couple of minutes they disappeared. I wiggled my eyebrows at James who just giggled.

"Can you show me this secret way out, without anyone knowing?"

"I might, but it'll cost you."

"You, young man, are on the same wave length as me." I hugged him close, feeling so much love for him I couldn't put into words.

"Where have you been all my life?"

"Right here, Molly," he laughed. "Right here."

"Well, James, you are my one true soul mate. Anything, and I mean anything, I can do for you, I'll be there. I love you so much. I'll be there, always."

We played in the pool for what seemed like hours. Micelle wandered up to the pool, shouting to James. "Out, James, time for you to dress for dinner."

Turning to me, he smiled. "Molly, you too. You have an hour to have a shower and change. Is there any reason you're fully clothed in the swimming pool or is this the new British beach wear fashion?

"Very witty, Micelle. I fell in and seeing I was already wet, it seemed pointless to get out to get changed and come back in. Plus, I didn't think your security guys would appreciate me stripping off to my Bridget Jones underwear."

He frowned. "Bridget who?"

"Never mind."

I shook my head, making my way to the pool steps while muttering to myself. I'm sure these people had no concept of TV or the movies. I climbed out and Micelle handed me a bath towel.

I gathered my belongings, depositing them on a table in the kitchen on my way through, not wanting them to get wet. I then made my way up to the bedroom.

I could hear the water running, so I assumed Jacob was having a shower. His jacket was hanging on a hook in the open wardrobe. The bathroom door was closed, so I tip-toed over.

I patted each pocket until I felt what could possibly be passports. Sure enough, in his inside pocket I struck gold.

Pulling them out, I quickly scanned each one until I found mine. Returning the rest, I kept mine and put it in the pocket of my case. Phase one complete.

Retrieving my phone, I sent a text to Alice.

Now my dear, need your passport number.

Why? She texted back.

Never mind, surprise!

My phone pinged again with the information I needed. The shower turned off and I hid my phone. Wrapping the towel tightly around me, I wiggled out of my wet clothes and sat on the edge of the bed, waiting for my turn in the shower.

Jacob came out of the bathroom and gave me a look. "Don't do that again," he said.

"Well, don't snatch my phone off me. That's just rude."

"Molly, I'm just trying to protect you."

"No, you were out of order. Subject closed." I brushed past him, closing the door to the bathroom behind me, locking it.

~~~~

I took my time showering. When I reentered the bedroom, Jacob had disappeared, again.

Wrapping the towel around me, I found a hair dryer in a drawer, tipped my hair upside down, drying it curly. I applied a small amount of makeup, as I didn't wear it much. My dad didn't like makeup, so I wasn't allowed to wear it growing up.

I found a pencil skirt in dark green and a white fitted blouse in the case I'd yet to unpack. I slipped on some black court shoes and I was ready for dinner.

As I was making my way down the stairs, James came barreling past.

"Hey, mister, stop. Wait for me."

He stopped, turned, and grabbed my hand. "Now then," I said, "don't you look smart? Who dressed you?"

"Daddy. He says everyone should dress for dinner."

"Did he now? Are we having guests?"

"No. I don't think so, Molly. Just Daddy, Alexander, Grandfather, and Jacob."

"Okay, sweetie. Lead the way."

We entered the dining room to find the men in deep conversation, which abruptly stopped.

"Carry on, don't let us interrupt."

Antonio stepped forward. "Molly, you look beautiful as always."

He enveloped me in a hug, kissing both of my cheeks. This I was struggling to get used to.

"James, you're growing up too fast. You're nearly a man." He shook his hand. God, he's a child for God's sake, hug him, I thought.

"Come, sit. Gentlemen, let's eat." Antonio led me to the table, pulling my chair out. Everyone else took their places for dinner.

Turning to Micelle I said, "I didn't smell anything cooking in the kitchen. Have you another one hidden somewhere?"

Micelle laughed. "No, our housekeeper is on his day off. I've organized the local restaurant to cook for us."

"You mean like a takeaway?"

Everyone looked in my direction. However, before anyone could respond, the connecting door to the kitchen opened. A young woman and man dressed in waiter's uniforms entered carrying trays of food.

"Not quite." Jacob turned to me and grinned.

I just raised my eyebrows, thanking the serving staff as each dish was placed on the table. As the last dish was served, James smiled at me. "Why do you keep saying thank you, Molly?"

"It's the English way of being polite, James. You must always remember your manners, it's what a woman admires in a man." I looked around the table, coughed and put my head down. James just giggled.

Wine was poured in our glasses, which of course Antonio had tested and acknowledged his agreement to the waiters. James launched into informing his dad of his school life and his hate of school, as all young boys do. So, my mind began to wander about the next day, and my collection of Alice from the airport. I'd zoned out and was picking at my plate of food when Alexander leaned over.

"Molly?"

"Mm, sorry. I was distracted."

"We have a business meeting tomorrow. It's unavoidable. Are you alright staying here with James? Eddie will be here."

"Yes, yes. That's fine."

Jacob leaned over, retrieving a dish, spooning a heap-full on my plate. "Eat."

I frowned at him. "I'm not hungry."

"Eat. You haven't eaten all day."

I continued to nibble at my food as the conversation continued around the table. What seemed like hours later, the plates had been cleared. Jacob stood, excused himself, then leaned down to me. Giving me a quick kiss, he whispered he had some calls to make.

Micelle stood. "James, do you want to show Molly were the TV room is? Perhaps you could both choose a movie to watch."

I jumped in before James could answer. "What about we go for a walk James, before it gets dark? It's cooler now and you can show me around."

"Okay, Molly, and when we come back, we can watch a movie before we go to bed."

"That's a plan, sweetie, let's go."

When we were out of hearing distance of the house, I turned to James. "So, can you show me the way out, without making it too obvious? I'm sure Micelle has camera's watching us."

"We could pretend to play hide and seek."

"Good idea, sweetie, if we start now, they'll soon lose interest in us."

We wandered around the grounds, each taking turns hiding. It was fun. We were both laughing and giggling. There were plenty of trees, bushes, and vines full of grapes waiting to be harvested.

Even though the sun was going down, we were still hot and sweaty from our game. James collapsed under a big tree and I flopped down next to him. We both lay there, looking into the sky.

"Molly, if you look behind you, you'll see some vines going up and over the wall."

I rolled over on my stomach, resting my chin on my hands. "I see them."

"If you walk in a straight line from this tree to the vines, there's a small door hidden behind it."

"And how would a very intelligent eight-year-old boy know this?"

James giggled. "Because my friend in the village told me. He's used it a couple of times when he's come to play with me."

"Interesting, didn't the security pick him up?"

"No because my other friends were here at the time. His mum doesn't like him coming here, so he sneaks in and then out again. No-one ever noticed."

"James, you're my kind of guy." We both laughed.

We made our way back to the house. James showed me into a massive room that housed a pool table, dart board, and a television. The screen was so big it would make our local cinema blush.

James made his way over to a large box near the TV, collecting three remotes on his way.

"I hope you know how to work that thing," I said, "because I'm hopeless with remotes. What's that box for?"

"It has all our films on it. What should we watch, Molly?"

"Have you ever seen The Golden Compass?"

"Do you think I'd like it?"

"I think you'd love it."

We both settled down on the huge leather sofa. The next minute, I felt a hand on my shoulder shaking me awake.

"Come on you two, time for bed."

Micelle lifted James up, throwing him over his shoulder. Jacob took my hand and helped me to stand. He turned everything off and we followed Micelle up the stairs to our room.

As the door closed behind us, he turned, pressing me against it. He held my face in his big hands as he bent down taking my lips, probing with his tongue. He stepped back, letting me come up for air.

"Are we talking again now?" I asked.

"We were never not talking. I was angry with you, plus I had a problem with something I was monitoring. Now, it's you and me time. Go and use the bathroom first, while I unpack." He turned me towards the bathroom, wrapped his arms around my waist, leaning in to nibble and kiss my neck. "Don't take too long."

~~~~

An hour later, wrapped in Jacob's arms, I heard his breathing even out in sleep. My brain was still on overload.

I should've told him about Alice's arrival, but I hadn't. I'd wanted to get Alice and I on a flight to Greece for a couple of days. That's why I'd asked for her passport number. However, the limited searches I'd done using my mobile app showed none were available.

I'd have to book us both into a hotel in town later. I didn't want to stay here. One, it wasn't my house, and two, it would be rather restricting. Girls should have fun.

I decided just before sleep claimed me, that I'd go with the flow tomorrow. The best laid plans always get mucked up anyway.

~~~~

The next morning, I woke up alone. I hadn't heard Jacob get up; however, I could smell his aftershave in the room, so he couldn't have been gone long.

I hurriedly found some clothes, brushed my teeth and brushed my hair, then followed the scent of freshly made coffee to the kitchen. Alexander and Jacob were putting their jackets on, Antonio was on his phone by the back door. Micelle was nowhere in sight.

"Morning, love, did you sleep well?" Jacob leaned in, kissing me. "I thought you could have a lie-in."

"Yes, I slept well, thanks. Are you going to be gone all day?"

"We plan to be, but things can always change. Would you like a coffee?"

"Please. Are all of you going?"

While Jacob was distracted, making my coffee, Alexander answered. "Yes, but don't worry. James has some friends coming over. The housekeeper should be here soon, so you can do your own thing. Eddie will be about if you should need anything, plus we're at the end of the phone in an emergency. Jon, the housekeeper, will cook you anything you want, just ask."

"Great, thank you," I answered as Antonio finished his call.

"Molly, good morning. I'm sorry, we must leave now but we'll see you later. We'll go out to dinner this evening." He reached for me, kissing each cheek, then collected his briefcase from a nearby chair. Alexander repeated the process.

"Stay out of trouble, sis," he grinned. He then followed Antonio out the door to the waiting SUV, leaving me alone with Jacob.

"Stay. Out. Of. Trouble." He pulled me into a hug and a sizzling kiss.

"I'm not a child, Jacob. Anyone would think I attract trouble."

"You do. And I know you're not a child, which I think I proved last night." He kissed me again, then was gone.

After they left, I helped myself to some toast and fresh coffee, making myself comfortable in the garden. I'd left my pencils and pad in the kitchen last night, so I retrieved them and waited for James to appear.

"Molly, has Daddy gone?"

"Morning, sweetie. Yes, about an hour or so ago. Would you like me to get you some breakfast?"

"No, I can ask Jon to make me some cereal. Would you like me to ask him to make you something?"

"No, sweetie, I've already had toast." I had to practically shout this at his retreating back as he ran to the kitchen. "James, don't run, you'll fall." God, I sounded like my mother.

About ten minutes later, James reappeared, followed by a very distinguished older man carrying a bowl of cereal.

"Molly, this is Jon. He looks after us."

I stood holding out my hand. "Please to meet you, Jon."

"A pleasure, my dear. Can I get you anything?"

"A cold drink would go down well."

"One cold drink coming up. Ice and lemon?"

"Yes please, thank you."

As Jon returned to the kitchen, I turned to James.

"James, what time are your friends arriving? I've to get to the airport for Alice's flight at three."

"Around lunch time."

"Do you think Jon will be distracted enough for me to go for a walk? If I can get to the village and a cash till, I can get a taxi to the airport in time. How long do you think it will take me to get to the village?"

"Mm, about ten minutes."

"Okay, as soon as your friends arrive, I'll wander off. Remember, it's our secret."

"Will I get in trouble?"

"No, sweetie, you'll be playing with your friends. As far as you know I've gone for a walk."

"Will you get into trouble, Molly?"

"Probably, but I'm a grown up, so I can do what I want." I ruffled his hair and grinned.

Just after one, James' friends started to arrive, either dressed in swimwear or carrying towels, which I assumed had swimwear inside. As they arrived, James introduced me.

Jon brought a tray of sandwiches and lemonade in a big jug. I laughed and shook my head at him.

"I take it this is a regular occurrence?"

"Yes, when the boy visits. He misses his friends. Can I get you something to eat or drink?"

"No, thank you. I was going to take a walk. It's a bit noisy for me."

"Okay, maybe when you come back."

"Yes, I'll pop my head in and let you know." With that he turned and returned to the kitchen.

Well, that was easy enough. I plugged in my headphones, finding some music on my mobile, and sliding on my sunglasses. I then wandered off, taking the same route as James and I made the previous evening.

As I approached the same tree I'd been shown, I sat down and leaned against it in the shade and rested a little. After about fifteen minutes, I thought I'd given whoever was watching the cameras enough time to lose interest in me.

I stood and made my way into the tree line, hidden from view. I made my way to the vines on the back wall, searching for the hidden door. I found it without any problem, opened it slightly and popped my head round, making sure there was no-one near. The coast was clear, so I slide through the gap, closing the door behind me.

I made my way to the road. I could see houses in the distance, so that's the direction I headed. Both sides of the road had grape vines growing in rows, the birds were singing, and the sun was shining. No traffic and no people, God, it felt good, as though I was the only one on the planet.

Sure, enough after five or ten minutes I rounded a bend and the first houses came in to view. The village was quaint and old, with flower boxes on windows in full bloom. I'd love to paint this. Retrieving my phone, I started snapping pictures.

I made my way through the town until I came upon a square full of shops and restaurants. I looked around, spotting a bank on the corner. It was closed, however there was a cash till in the wall.

Making my way over, I inserted my card and punched in my pin, all the time hoping it would work and give me the much-needed money to get a taxi to the airport. It was siesta time obviously, as there seemed to be no one around. The machine spat out my money, thank God.

I pocketed the money, turning in a circle. I needed to ask someone where I could hire a taxi. A couple of the restaurants seemed to be open, so I made for the nearest one to ask for directions. I stepped through the doorway.

"Hello!" I shouted.

"Ciao, posso aiutarti."

"Sorry, do you speak English?"

"A little. Can I help you?" an elderly gentleman answered.

"I was looking for a taxi to take me to the airport."

"It is siesta. You'll have to wait until four o'clock. Can I get you something to drink?"

"Oh dear, I have to meet a flight at three thirty. I might miss my friend."

"You look familiar, my dear. Do I know you? I forget these things in my old age."

"I don't think so, it's my first visit; however, you might know my brothers, Alexander and Micelle."

"Ah, you have the look of Francesca. Beautiful lady."

"My mother, you knew her?"

"Of course. Come, I'll give you refreshment, then I'll take you to meet your friend."

"That's very nice of you. I'll pay you for your time and the fuel."

"We'll see. Sit."

The old gentleman disappeared, returning ten minutes later with two espressos and a slice of cake. He sat opposite me and watched me eat the delicious confectionary.

"Oh my, this is good. I bake cakes in England for my village shop. I'd love the recipe, if it's not a family secret that is," I laughed.

"For you, I might share. What brings you here, my dear?"

"My father and brother decided I needed a vacation."

"You're at the villa? Why do they not take you to the airport to pick up your friend?"

"Long story short, they're out on business. I didn't want to bother them."

He shook his head. "I think your father has his hands full with you, little one. Drink up. I'll lock up and fetch the car. It will take us about twenty minutes, you'll be there in time for your friend."

I frowned. Why does everyone keep saying that?

We climbed in an old pickup truck that had seen better days. I turned to my driver and smiled.

"Molly, my name's Molly. Thank you so much for doing this for me."

"Luis, and it's my pleasure. It is not every day I get to take a ride with a beautiful young woman, not at my time of life anyway. I'd have liked to have a daughter. However, I was only blessed with sons."

"How many sons?"

"Five, all strapping lads, but sadly, no daughter."

"Why did you stop?" I laughed.

"No more bedrooms."

We both laughed. Luis then focused again on the road as signs for the airport came into view.

"Would you like me to wait for you and your friend?"

"Gosh no, I'm a bit early, plus she'll have to go through passport control." I pulled some money from my pocket. "Let me pay you for the fuel and your time."

He reached out putting his hand on top of my hand to stop me. "No, bring your friend to my restaurant, meet my sons. They're all single."

I laughed out loud, opening the door, accidently dropping a couple of notes on the floor as I climbed out.

"Thank you, Luis. I'll see you soon." Little did I know how soon.

~~~~

I entered the airport, making my way to the information board. Checking the flight was on time, which it was, I made my way to the nearest café. I bought a tea, sitting in a booth near the front so I could people watch. I waited for Alice's flight to land.

Do you ever sit and watch people, wondering where there going, whether its business or pleasure? Do they live here, or are they visiting?

In no time at all, it was time to make my way to Arrivals. People hugging and kissing as they met their loved ones as they came through the electric doors. It wasn't long before I spied Alice, coming through the doors, dragging a small case on wheels.

"Alice! Alice! Here." She looked over and smiled, waving. We hugged and kissed, not letting go.

"God, Molly, it seems ages since we've seen each other. We've got a lot of catching up to do. Where are we heading? Why are you wearing a hat and sunglasses, are you in disguise?"

"Long story, which I'll get to."

Just then I felt a tap on my shoulder. I turned to find a big muscly chest in my eyeline. I looked up from the chest to see Kade's face, looking down at me. "Bloody hell."

His big hands removed my hat and sunglasses. "Molly, I thought it was you. Where's Jacob?"

"Meeting."

"Eddie?"

"Watching James and his friends."

"Right, so who's with you?"

"Alice, my friend."

"Alice was on the same flight as me. So, who brought you to the airport and why are they not with you now?"

"Luis gave me a lift. I don't need a babysitter, thank you. What are you doing here anyway?"

"Who the hell is Luis? How are you getting back to the villa?"

I sighed in frustration. "Never you mind, and Luis is my friend."

"You've only been here a day. How did you meet your new friend, and what about introducing me to this friend?"

Alice had been standing silently behind me, taking in the exchange.

"Alice, this is Kade. Kade, this is Alice. Now what are you doing here?"

"Vacation."

"Which just happens to be here? Now isn't that a coincidence?"

"Come on, ladies, I have transport. I'll get you home."

"That's not necessary, Kade."

"Oh yes it is, sweetheart." With that he grabbed Alice's case and my arm. I turned, looking at Alice who was grinning and shaking her head. I just rolled my eyes.

~~~~

Kade deposited us in the back of guess what? Yes, you have it, another SUV with a very memorable number plate.

"This car is familiar," I said.

"It's from the estate. Jacob left it earlier."

"That means he knew you were coming and never mentioned it to me?" Kade ignored my question, a phone dialing came through the speakers.

"Kade, you've landed?" Jacob's voice answered.

"Have you lost something?"

Silence. "No, not that I'm aware."

"A five foot nothing pocket rocket, with auburn curly hair?"

"Molly, damn it, where are you and how did you get there?"

I folded my arms and looked out of the window silently. Alice coughed and leaned forward.

"Jacob, it's Alice, she was collecting me from the airport."

"Alice, I didn't know you were coming, I'd have come and got you. Molly, speak to me. Why was I not told about Alice's visit and more importantly than that, how did you get out of the villa without alerting the security?"

"No comment."

"Molly, it's your father. Take your friend back to the house. I'll arrange for Jon to make ready one of the spare rooms. We'll discuss this later. I refuse to embarrass your friend by the fallout of your actions."

"That's not necessary, we can book in a hotel. Alice is only here for four days. We want to have fun, not be stuck behind four walls."

There was a burst of angry Italian in the background.

"Can you please speak English?"

Kade laughed. "I really don't think you need to know what was said. Needless to say, you're in big trouble."

Jacob came back on. "Molly, go to the villa, relax with your friend. We have dinner reservations for eight, Alice is invited, so give yourselves time to get ready. Kade, your room is ready, we'll meet you and the girls at the restaurant." With that he was gone.

I turned to Alice, she mimed the hot sign and pointed in Kade's direction. I nodded and laughed.

~~~~

The journey back to the villa took no time at all. As we pulled up near the gates, they opened automatically, allowing Kade to pull to the front of the villa where Eddie was waiting for us. He had a frown on his face. As the car stopped, he leaned in, opening my door.

"Miss Molly, how the hell did you get to the airport? You do know you've landed me in deep water? Jacob is probably going to sack me."

"Chill, Eddie, I'll speak to Jacob. Come and meet my friend Alice."

Kade had jumped out and opened the other door, helping Alice out. Kade nodded at Eddie and opened the boot to retrieve Alice's hand luggage.

"Alice, this is Eddie, my friend." Turning to Eddie. "Eddie, meet Alice."

"I've heard a lot about you, Miss Alice. I'm very pleased to meet you, although I've a feeling I'll be in a lot of trouble for not personally collecting you from the airport. As I'm sure Molly well knows."

Eddie grabbed the case from Kade, they shook hands and moved forward into the villa.

I linked Alice's elbow. "Come on in. I'll find out what room you're in, then we can change and go sit by the pool; I'm sure its G & T time somewhere." We giggled like kids and followed the men in.

Jon met us at the bottom of the stairs. "I've put Miss Alice in the room next to yours," he said, addressing me. He turned to Kade shaking his hand. "Nice to see you again, Kade. You are in your normal room."

I raised my eyebrows at Kade. "So, Kade, you come here often?" He just laughed and continued up the stairs.

"Come on, Alice, let's get you settled." We followed until we arrived at Alice's room. As soon as the door closed behind us, Alice dropped her case and turned to me.

"Wow! Just wow. Kade is one hot, hot guy. If you're not sleeping with him, this Jacob must be pretty awesome."

I threw my head back and laughed. "God, I missed you. Wait until you meet my father and brothers," I said raising my hands to sign inverted commas. "In fact, Antonio is pretty fit for his age."

We grinned at each other. "Lead the way, girlfriend."

~~~~

We changed quickly and made our way to the pool. I expected James and his friends to be playing but the pool area was empty.

There was, however, two long drinks with ice and lemon by the sun loungers, shaded by an umbrella.

"Oh my God, Jon is on the ball. If I'm not mistaken that's our gin and tonics." We both collapsed on to a sun bed and grabbed our drinks.

"Right," Alice said. "Start at the beginning and don't leave a thing out. I want to be clued up before this meal tonight."

Two gin and tonics later, Alice was up to speed. "Wow! You don't do things in half measures, girlfriend. I have to say, Kade is one hot guy and he has a sense of humor. If I wasn't happily married, he could turn my duvet down any day."

"Talking of which, I wonder where he's disappeared to?" I sat up and looked around the pool area. Just then Eddie appeared.

"Eddie, where's Kade gone?"

"He's taking some calls in the office. It's six o'clock. Are you girls not getting ready to go out?"

"Yes, I suppose we should make a move. Is James coming with us?"

"No, he's gone to his friend's for tea."

"Is that allowed?"

"Yes, Miss Molly, he has security with him. This isn't a prison camp, you're allowed out. However, telling us were you're going is important, we're only thinking of your safety."

"That's all very well, Eddie. Until a couple of months ago, I could go where I liked, when I liked. So, I'm sorry if I missed the memo."

Eddie shook his head and laughed. "You, Miss Molly, are trouble with a capital T. You'll be the death of me, either that or the cause of me hitting the unemployment line. Come on, give me your glasses. I'll return them to the kitchen while you go and get dressed."

"Are you coming with us?" I asked turning back to him.

"No, Kade's taking you, the restaurant is only in the village."

I turned to Alice. "Well, this is going to be interesting, especially if the restaurant is owned by Luis, my new friend." We both laughed.

One and a half hours later, with my hair straightened by Alice, wearing a black sleeveless pencil dress and minimal makeup, I was ready. Alice was dressed to impress wearing an emerald green dress which flattered her slim figure and showed off one shoulder and arm.

"You look stunning," I said. "Anyone would think you're trying to pull tonight," I laughed. "Did they run out of material; you seem to have a sleeve missing."

She swatted me with her hand. "Cheeky, it's supposed to look sophisticated."

We both laughed and grabbed our purses, making our way down to the bottom floor.

"Wow! Ladies, you both look stunning," Kade said, meeting us at the bottom of the stairs. "It's a shame I've to share you with four other males."

"You're such a smoothie, Kade. I bet you say that to all your dates."

"Only the ones I want to take home at the end of the evening."

"You do realise that Alice is happily married with a child?"

Alice piped up behind me. "Molly, stop telling everyone I'm married, you're ruining my street cred."

~~~~

The journey to the restaurant didn't take long and of course it was Luis'. I smiled and winked at Alice, who smirked back at me. We were like sisters; we could always tell what the other one was thinking.

As Kade parked, he told us to stay where we were until he opened the doors for us. He locked the car with his fob and herded us towards the entrance. He was in the middle of us, his hand on the base of our backs. I was also sure he was doing it to wind a certain someone up because he was smirking as we entered the restaurant.

As soon as we entered, Luis spotted me. Like a true Italian, he was barreling towards us, hands in the air, speaking Italian. He took me by the shoulders giving me a huge hug and kissing both cheeks, turning to Alice, he did the same.

Changing to English, he said "Molly, you look beautiful. You found your friend? This is good. I've plenty of sons to go around."

"Luis, this is Alice and Kade our FRIEND." I made a point of emphasizing the word. "We're meeting my father and brothers for dinner."

"Yes, yes, he's at his normal table. Come, I'll escort you."

As it happens, Luis was beaten to the post, as Jacob was striding towards us like a man on a mission.

"Molly!" He leaned in for a kiss and stepped back. "We'll talk later about your little disappearing act. Now introduce me to your friend."

I turned to Alice. "Alice, this is Jacob."

Alice stepped forward to shake his hand. "Nice to meet you. To say I've heard a lot about you is a bit of an understatement."

Jacob laughed, turning to Kade. "Kade." He nodded and shook his hand.

Jacob reached for my hand and turned us towards the table where the others were waiting.

Introductions were then performed all around. When everyone was seated, and menus were handed out, Antonio leaned forward.

"Ladies, would you like me to order for you? Or would you prefer that I read you the menu, so you can make your own choices?"

"I've a better idea," I said. "Excuse me, Luis, what would you recommend?"

"For you, Molly, I'll prepare a selection of the house dishes for you to try."

I turned to Antonio, who nodded his agreement, as did everyone else.

"That would be very kind of you, Luis. Thank you."

Turning to Antonio, he asked, "Would you like your usual wine choice?"

"Yes, Luis, unless the ladies would prefer something other than red wine?" He raised his eyebrow in our direction.

We only shook our heads. I assumed that, being Italian, and rich, he'd know his wines.

"One more thing, Luis, before you go. How do you know my daughter so well?"

"Did Miss Molly not tell you? I made sure she arrived at the airport safely to collect her friend." With that he turned and left. I felt six pairs of eyes all focused on me, and I blushed.

I coughed, "Right, well that cleared that up then. It's good to have friends in the restaurant trade, don't you think?"

Alexander winked at me and smirked, as the waiter appeared with our wine. After our glasses were filled, Antonio raised his glass in a toast.

"To family and friends, old and new."

The wine was superb. Everyone settled down and started on the assorted meats and olives that appeared in front of us.

"What are you up to tomorrow, ladies?" Micelle asked.

"I thought we could go to the beach for the day. Alice can drive a moped, so I thought it would be good to hire one and go exploring."

"No, absolutely not," Jacob butted in.

"Who died and put you in charge? If I say I'm going to the beach, then I'm going to the beach."

"It's not the beach that's the problem. It's you on the back of a bike, that's the problem. Especially as you create havoc on two feet, never mind on two wheels."

"Now you're just being rude. I'm not that bad."

Alice couldn't contain her laughter.

Turning to her. "And you're supposed to be my best friend."

"He does have a valid point," she laughed. "Considering he doesn't know you as well as I do."

"We'll see. I'm sure we'll be fine, seeing as you're in charge. Plus, I'm sure we'll have an armed escort wherever we go." I looked over at Antonio, who nodded his agreement.

"You don't have to hire your transport; we have such a thing at the villa. However, Molly, Alice, I'd like your absolute promise that you'll remain within sight of Eddie and whoever we send with him to make sure you have a safe and trouble-free day. We'll be at the villa and easily contactable all day."

I looked over at Jacob, who frowned and looked at Kade, who shook his head.

After that, the main meal was served and the topic of conversation turned more general. Micelle and Alexander interrogated Alice about her family and her work, moving the conversation along until they knew everything about the both of us and our friendship.

I listened and watched as my brothers openly flirted with my best friend. I'd have to remind her that she was married later.

~~~~

The meal was excellent, as I knew it would be. Micelle went and settled the bill, while the rest of us thanked Luis for his hospitality. We were then hustled out to the SUVs. Alice and I returned to Kade's.

As I reached for the door handle, Jacob pulled me back, opening it for me and helping me climb in. I looked over at Alice to see Kade doing the gentlemanly thing for her as well. It made me smile. I'm not a women's libber, I love to have doors opened for me and my chair pulled out.

When we reached the villa, we had unfortunately missed James; he had fallen asleep whilst watching TV, which was a shame, I so wanted Alice to meet him.

TWENETY-FOUR

The next morning was warm and sunny. I wandered down to the kitchen after knocking on Alice's door and getting no answer. As I approached the kitchen, I could hear male voices.

Jacob, Micelle, and James were entertaining Alice at breakfast, it seems I'd slept in and missed the bus.

"Morning, everyone, have I missed breakfast?"

Jacob jumped up, kissing me soundly on the lips and holding the chair out for me. Jon came behind me, placing a plate full of cooked meats, cheeses, and freshly baked bread in front of me.

"Thank you, Jon. Alice and I are going to the beach today. Would we have anything to take with us for lunch?"

"Of course, Molly. I'll put something together for you."

I leaned over to James. "Morning, James. I see you've met my friend Alice. She has a son your age."

"I know, Molly, she said she'll bring him next time so we can become friends."

"That's a great idea. What are you doing today?"

"I'm going out with dad for the day."

Micelle ruffled his hair. "He's sprouting up. I think we'll need to get him some new clothes that fit."

"Molly, I'm not happy about you and Alice going to the beach on the bike. For a start you don't like bikes. You wouldn't go on the back of Kade's."

"We'll be fine, Jacob. Eddie will be watching us, and I'm sure Alice will go slowly. Besides, Alice is a pro on a scooter."

"Yes, but I bet she's never had you on the back before."

"Chill, Jacob. Go and do what you do. We'll see you tonight."

He leaned in, kissing me. "Ring me if you need me."

I turned to Alice. "What time do you want to leave?"

"After you've eaten is fine."

"We can ask Eddie to take our picnic, umbrella and towels. That leaves my arms free to hang on to you for dear life. You know what you're doing, don't you? And you won't go too fast?"

Alice laughed. "Piece of cake."

~~~~

Thirty minutes later, we were ready. Alice was familiarizing herself with the little blue moped. I had on my straw hat, sunglasses and a bright orange rubber ring with a duck's head on the front.

Eddie climbed out of the driver's seat of the SUV that had been assigned to us for the day. He rounded the boot, shaking his head and laughing.

"What the hell do you need a rubber ring for? You can swim. That hat isn't going to save your brain if you come off that bike. Come on, Molly, let me take you in the car. If anything happens to you, my life is over."

I made a puffing sound. "Eddie, this is a girly day that you, I might add, are gate-crashing. Now stop fussing."

He turned, shaking his head once again, mumbling.

I turned to Alice. "Are we ready?"

"Yes. Now, Molly, listen very carefully to what I say, unless you want to make Jacob's fears a reality. Hold on tight. If I bend to the left or right, you copy what I do. After ten minutes you'll be a natural."

"I'll be honest, Alice, Jacob was right. I'm frightened to death. However, it's on my wish list, so let's do this. Oh, and if you ever tell my brothers or Jacob that I nearly lost my nerve. You're dead."

We both climbed on the bike and off we went with Eddie in slow pursuit. Alice was right, ten minutes later, I was in sync with her movements. It felt so freeing to have the wind in my hair and surrounded by beautiful green vineyards for miles.

"Do we know where you're going?" I asked Alice.

"I'm following the signs. You know, the ones that say this way to the beach?"

"Oh right, good idea   ."

I grinned to myself. It was so good to have someone else in charge for once.

~~~~

After about thirty minutes and no sign of the sea, I was beginning to get a bit worried. The next minute, the SUV with Eddie at the wheel overtook us and pulled up in front of us. Both him and his partner climbed out. We came to a stop on the side of the road.

"Do you two know where you're going, or are we going joy ride all day?"

"We're following the signs. It's not our fault someone's altered them, leading us on a wild goose chase."

"Right, follow us," said Mr. Moody, which was my name for the man. We'd never been formally introduced; however, I swear I'd never seen the man smile once in my company. I got the feeling he didn't approve of me.

Alice spoke up, elbowing me in the stomach. "Good idea, James, lead the way." We both looked at each other and laughed. We climbed aboard and followed our escort detail.

Mr. Moody took us to a picturesque little beach. Not a soul was about. As Alice parked the bike, Eddie reached in the boot for our picnic basket, umbrella and towels.

"Right, ladies, where would you like to set up?"

Alice, as usual, took charge. "Over near those rocks, please. Molly burns so she needs shade." She plonked the straw hat on my head, I frowned, then followed her to said rocks.

After making sure we had everything we needed, Eddie returned to the car, where Mr. Moody was on his mobile. Alice and I laid out the beach towels. Sitting cross legged, we faced each other and tucked into the delights of our picnic basket.

An ice-cold bottle of champagne, two glasses, and strawberries took pride of place at the very top. Underneath sat an assortment of cheeses, fresh bread, cold meats, and a freshly tossed Italian salad.

"Mm, delicious. God, this is the life, Molly. I think we have just joined the group of ladies that lunch."

I laughed out loud. Leaning back, I wiggled out of my shorts and top, stretching out to sunbathe.

"What factor have you got on? You know how you burn."

"Stop fussing. Jacob rubbed factor fifty on me before we left."

"I bet he did." We both laughed and settled down. "Did you get the third degree about yesterday?"

"Some, but I pacified him."

"I bet you did."

~~~~

A couple of hours later, I was hot and bored. We had chatted awhile, then Alice started reading and I sat and watched the horizon as a large boat anchored five or six hundred yards out.

"Nice boat out there, bet that cost a packet," I said to Alice, not taking my eyes off the boat in question.

"I wonder what type of person owns it?" she replied.

"Maybe if I zoom in with my phone, I could see who's on board. I know, we should have a wager. Young or old?"

"Young or old what?"

"Do you think the owner is young or old?"

Alice sat up to inspect further. "Young."

"You think? I think older, with a twenty-five-year-old girlfriend. Sugar daddy."

We shook hands. "Hang on. What are we betting for?"

"An I.O.U."

"Done."

I rooted in my beach bag for my phone, punching in my pin, I then zoomed in with the camera app.

It took a minute to adjust the picture setting. Eventually, two male faces came into view.

"Oh my," I said. "That's so not good. That is really, really, bad."

"What, don't tell me you know the people on the boat?"

"Unfortunately, yes, and it's not good. I need to send a photo of this to Jacob."

"Who is it?"

"Well, one is Kincaid senior and the other is Antonio's accountant." My phone pinged as the photo sent, and as my mobile started to ring, I turned to see Mr. Moody making his way down to us.

"Jacob."

"I take it you're still at the beach?"

"Yes, why?"

"You need to collect your things and head back. Use the car rather than the bike."

"I don't see why. They don't know I saw them."

"No, they didn't; however, Kincaid knows you're here. We have a mole, high up in our organization. It's safe to say Kincaid knows where you are. If he knows, so does Ryan. Please, just once will you listen, and do what I ask?"

I thought about it, as Mr. Moody pulled the towel from under me. Throwing my shorts and t-shirt in the direction of my head, I glared at him.

"Okay, Jacob, we're on our way back now." I disconnected and growled in Mr. Moody's direction.

"Are you this nice to everyone or are you giving me some kind of special treatment?" I could hear Alice stifling a laugh.

"I'm not paid to be nice; I'm paid to keep you breathing." He turned and made his way to the car with our things.

I turned to Alice, who was still trying to hide her laughter. "He's a dick, I don't like him."

"Ha ha, I think he's received the postcard."

We returned to the car, where Eddie helped us in. Mr. Moody removed his jacket and tie, threw them in the boot, then mounted the moped which roared to life.

"Home, James," I shouted from the back seat. Eddie just shook his head and laughed. At least he had a sense of humor.

~~~~

We arrived back at the villa in no time, both Alice and I jumping out before Eddie could get the doors. Jacob was making his way down the front stairs.

"Ladies, pack your things, we're returning home. Alice you're with us. When you're ready for home, I'll make arrangements to get you there." Jacob walked towards me, wrapping an arm around my shoulders and tucking me into his side.

"Why are we flying back early? I thought we were going to an occasion of some sort?"

"Plans have changed. We have to contain the damage to the business, but more importantly, I have to neutralize Ryan Kincaid. I refuse to be looking over my shoulder, wondering whether or not he's going to take you and disappear."

Alice had gone on ahead. Jacob maneuvered me up the steps.

"I have some things to sort out. You and Alice pack, have a shower, and change. We'll have dinner with your father, James and Micelle, then catch our ride home."

"Oh? Are Antonio and James not coming with us?"

"No, just you and Alice."

"But you're coming?"

"Yes, with Eddie and Joshua."

I scrunched my nose up. "Joshua?"

"Yes." He turned me round to face Mr. Moody.

Oh no! Just what the party needed, I thought. This was going to be one bumpy ride home.

186

Jacob kissed me, then pushed me towards Alice. We headed straight for the staircase and our rooms.

"What was all that about?" Alice asked.

"You, girlfriend, are going to see my new house and meet Missy. You'll love her, seeing as you're a cat person."

"You didn't look too happy before when you screwed your face up."

"That might've been when Jacob informed me that Mr. Moody was coming too. Did you know his name is Joshua?"

Alice just laughed, entering her room and closing the door.

I busied myself packing, then laid my travelling clothes out on the bed. I headed to the bathroom to run a bath. I heard a door closing; Jacob must have sorted out what he had to do in record time.

I leaned over the tub to check the water temperature. "Just having a quick soak, Jacob, won't be long." My breath caught as I felt someone behind me. One hand went around my waist, the other covered my mouth.

"You don't have to go to all that trouble on my behalf," Ryan whispered in my ear. I started to struggle. However, he held me tight against his body.

"Stop struggling. I won't hurt you. We're just going to take a little trip."

I closed my eyes. God, not again, I thought as blackness descended.

TWENETY-FIVE

What is it with people wanting to knock me out?

My eyes were heavy. I could hear male voices arguing around me; however, for some reason, my eyelids would not cooperate. I recognized Ryan's voice and his father's. The other was familiar, but no name was jumping out at me. I flexed my legs and arms.

"She's coming around," the voice I didn't recognize said.

"Molly, open your eyes for me, sweetheart."

I could feel Ryan's breath on me, so he had to be knelt in front of me or leaning over me.

I tried again, opening my eyes that is. It took me a couple of minutes to focus.

"You, you weasel. I knew I recognized that voice."

"Why did you bring her here? Now she knows my involvement."

"Because you're expendable and my use for you has expired. Once a traitor, always a traitor." With that Kincaid senior reached behind his back. He pulled out a gun with what I knew was a silencer, I'd seen it on the TV. He held it against the accountant's head and pulled the trigger.

I curled in a ball. I was so shocked, I couldn't cry, or speak. I just began to shake.

"Did you have to do that in front of her?" Ryan asked, turning to his father.

"Your obsession with this woman is unnatural. I'm beginning to think you also are becoming a liability. I should never have tasked you with keeping an eye on her for the last few years."

With that he turned the gun on Ryan and pulled the trigger. Blood and brain matter rained down on me.

"Oh my God, you shot your son. How could you kill your own blood?" I shouted.

I'm so dead, he's cleaning house. I was next, I could feel it. I looked down at the blood and gore that covered me and started to scream uncontrollably.

"Stop screaming, now. Don't worry, I've plans for you, little lady." He smirked, then slapped me so hard my head bounced off the wall. I was so shocked and disoriented that my screaming stopped, and sobs took over. I heard Kincaid senior shouting to someone to come and clean the mess up.

"Why are you doing this?" I asked between sobs.

"Money and power. I've a leak somewhere and my export routes are being targeted and closed down. So, with the help of him, he turned and nodded at the dead accountant, I've rerouted my products through legitimate pathways, your father's. Somehow, your boyfriend has gotten wind of this. Now, you're my bargaining tool. Without your stalker, that being my son, maybe I can get everything back on track."

"You're one very sick man."

I turned into the wall, curling back up into a ball, and closed my eyes. Please, Jacob, find me, I don't want to die.

I heard and felt someone moving around the cabin cleaning up;

however, I closed my mind, taking myself into a room in my head and locking the door.

~~~~

Hours later, I could hear the humming of the engine. I lifted an eyelid and noted the cabin was dark. No movement and no voices; I was alone.

I turned over and straightened out. I wasn't tied up, for which I was grateful. I desperately needed the bathroom. I let my eyes adjust to the darkness, then swung my legs around to try and stand. I felt dirty and sticky.

Trying to avoid any mirrors as I didn't think my stomach could survive the sight of my body covered in Ryan's blood, I made my way to the bathroom, closed the door and relieved myself.

After washing my hands, I used the water to wash as much as I could off my face and arms, then made my way back into the cabin. I moved to a clean spot, resting my chin on my knees as I waited.

~~~~

Hours seemed to pass by. I was beginning to think I'd been left alone on the boat, when suddenly I could hear feet moving on deck, followed by shouts and pops like guns being fired.

I lifted my head, turning it, straining my ears. I was wrestling with the idea of attempting to get someone's attention by hammering on the door. But then, on second thought, what if it wasn't Jacob or Alexander? I could be jumping from the pot to the fire. No perhaps I should hide, try and escape later.

I crept to the bathroom, shut the shower curtain, and made myself into the smallest ball ever, and waited. I heard someone kick the door open to the main cabin. Holding my breath, I tried to keep my body from shaking. Doors to cupboards were opened and I could hear muttered curses.

"Molly, damn it, where the hell are you?"

Was that Jacob? I couldn't tell. I was paralyzed with fear. I so didn't want to die. The door to the bathroom opened.

"Molly! Molly! Are you in here?"

"Jacob? Oh my God, yes I'm here."

The tears started; I just couldn't stop them. The shower curtain was pulled opened. His two strong arms reached for me as he sank to the floor and pulled me into his lap.

"Shit. For a second there I thought I'd lost you. You're covered in blood. Are you hurt?"

All I could do was shake my head and cling onto him, pressing so close. I wished his body could absorb mine and take everything I'd seen in the last couple of hours away like a bad dream.

Everything seemed to happen at once. I was lifted out of Jacob's arms, but I didn't release my strangle hold from his neck.

"Molly, let go sweetheart, its Joshua. He won't hurt you."

"Mr. Moody, he doesn't like me. I want to stay with you."

"Who said I didn't like you? I think you're a pain in the butt, that's all."

I looked at Jacob, who lifted an eyebrow and smothered a grin. I released my grip, letting Joshua carry me up to the upper deck. Two small craft were anchored to the side of the bigger boat. Jacob jumped aboard one and Joshua handed me over to him.

"Clean up here and keep me up-to-date. I need to get Molly out of here and checked over. Once that's done, meet us at the jet, we're going home."

Joshua's only response was a chin lift. Not sure what that meant, it must be a man thing. The speed boat took off, Jacob smothered me in blankets, holding my head into his neck. The next thing, I was being lifted into a SUV, Alexander was driving.

"She okay?"

"Yes, just in shock. I need to get her warm and into some clean clothes. Then home."

"Right! Everyone's ready. Antonio has taken Alice out of the way for some last-minute shopping. She thinks Molly's resting with a headache. By the time they return, we'll be good to go. Micelle will handle things this end."

I could hear them talking but stayed quiet. My eyelids began to feel heavy, plus the heat coming from Jacob and the motion of the car, made me feel as though I could sleep for a week.

~~~~

The next thing I knew, I was being lifted from the car by Alexander and handed back to Jacob. He kissed my forehead and snuggled me close, striding up the stairs to our room.

"Molly, I'm going to get you in the shower. You're cold and in shock. After that, we'll get you dressed and then we're going back to England."

"I want to go home."

"I know, sweetheart, I'm taking you home."

"No, I want to go home with Alice."

Standing in front of me, taking my face in his hands, he leaned in close, making me look into his eyes.

"Molly, you know that's no longer an option. Everyone knows you're Antonio's daughter. Although Kincaid is no longer a threat, your father has upset a lot of people through the years. You must stay with the family now, it's the only way. Plus, you are mine – you're in my heart, in my mind, I can't stop thinking of you. I love you so much. I want to marry you so that everyone will know you're taken. I know how you feel about the estate and living there. We can live in the cottage. I'll ramp up the security so you won't be in danger when I'm not around. I know you're in shock now. Let me take care of you, get you home, then you can make plans. Okay?"

I looked him in the eye and nodded. He leaned in and kissed me.

EPILOGUE

The journey home was quiet and quick. We arrived back at the estate without incident, but that didn't surprise me. The Kincaid issue was no longer a problem. As Jacob stopped the SUV, I realised where we were.

"Jacob, I'd like to go to the cottage, please. Alice and I'll be staying there."

He ignored me, stepping out of the car, striding around the vehicle and opening my door.

"I know, sweetheart. I'm just collecting Zeuss and Missy."

"Oh."

Turning to Alice, I raised my eyebrows and smiled.

~~~~

The guys were ecstatic to see me. Zuess jumped so high his head came higher than mine. And Missy wove between my legs, meowing. God, it was so good to be home again. I gave Alice the grand tour; she loved it.

~~~~

"What are you going to do, Molly?" We were standing in the kitchen with a night cap.

"Jacob has asked me to marry him. Plus, there is the fact that I'm the daughter of an Italian mafia boss."

194

Alice laughed. "You do exaggerate. He's a very nice man. You just have to give him a chance, and your brothers. Well, wow! Speaking of wow, what's happened to Kade?"

"Jacob said he was staying in Italy for a bit, some business problems. They're very vague about what exactly they do."

"And Jacob, he vanished pretty quickly."

"He locked us in and set the alarms, he said he'd be back in an hour."

"So, with the risk of repeating myself. What are you going to do?"

"I want to be normal again; however, I'm realistic enough to know that's not going to happen. I have feelings for Jacob. I'm not sure it's love yet, but it could be. It's early days. I think I'll stay and see where this thing goes. Marriage though, not yet."

"Ha ha! Good luck with that, Jacob is a very driven man as far as you're concerned."

"We'll see." We raised our glasses.

"Cheers!"

"To the future and all it brings."

The End for Now!

ABOUT THE AUTHOR

Hi, I'm J. B. Dunlop (Jeanette Ellmer) and I'm very much a romantic. My motto in life has always been: "It's character building." I'm a mother, and grandmother (Blue Nan) to four very special grandchildren.

Godparent to many and I love them all.

This book is for me, something I said I would do when I was at school.

On my wish list and I wouldn't have done it without Bret's help. Thank you, thank you, thank you.

Comments and questions are always welcome.
Email the author at jbdunlop22@hotmail.com

Printed in Great Britain
by Amazon

36263155R00121